PRAISE FOR MARK OF THE LEAST

"A wildly original and magical twist on the Robin Hood narrative, Kendra Merritt's *By Wingéd Chair* is packed to the spokes with complex characters, wry humor, and flawless world building."

-Darby Karchut, best-selling author of DEL TORO MOON and FINN FINNEGAN

"With a wonderfully crafted blend of swords and sorcery and characters based on Robin Hood, Merritt tops this story off with the lead character readers need nowadays; a strong, independent, powerful female mage who also happens to be in a wheelchair. Readers will be constantly turning pages to see what happens next to this fun group of characters through the twists and turns they won't see coming."

-The Booklife Prize

"Kendra Merritt's prose is fresh, with one-line descriptions that crack like a whip, and she doesn't miss an opportunity to surprise the reader. From the first line to the last, I was enchanted with *By Winged Chair*."

-Todd Fahnestock, best-selling author of FAIRMIST and THE WISHING WORLD

ALSO BY KM MERRITT

Mishap's Heroes Series

Magic and Misrule

Death and Devotion

Trust and Treason

Illusions and Infamy

Sparks and Scales

Wastelands and War

Mark of the Least Novels

By Wingéd Chair

Skin Deep

Catching Cinders

Shroud for a Bride

A Matter of Blood

Mark of the Least Shorts

After the Darkness

When Quiet Comes to Call

Aria at the Opera

A Galadon Exile

Blood and Hope (in the *Fantastic Realms* anthology)

Faire-Weather Magic (in the *Wild* anthology)

Chasing Waves (in the *Girls of Might and Magic* anthology)

MISHAP'S HEROES

1/2

Creation and Calamity

KM MERRITT

BLUE FYRE PRESS

Blue Fyre Press: bluefyrepress@gmail.com

First Edition

ISBN: 978-1-951009-27-4

Cover Art: Lucy Lin

Created with Vellum

PART ONE
VOLA

Vola's origin story is best read after *Magic and Misrule.*

ONE

VOLA SWUNG HER AX, a hand-me-down from her mother, chopping the last goblin's head clean off his shoulders. It rolled down the hill away from the cave mouth and stopped at the feet of a massive orc dressed in a fur-lined loincloth and a leather harness. He leaned on his greatsword and propped his foot on the goblin's head.

"There, see, now you've got the feel of it," he said with a wide grin. "Just remember to keep your weight on your toes."

"And remember to clean your blade afterward." A short lithe woman with bushy roan-colored hair placed her boot on a dead goblin's back and yanked her own ax out of its spinal cord.

"You know when normal people go on family camping trips they don't make detours to wipe out the local pests," Vola said, stooping to clean her weapon. Her mother might have been the deadliest woman east of Firewatch, but she was also a real stickler for cleanliness.

"I thought we were having fun," Lydia Battlemane said, stopping to pout at Vola.

Vola sighed and rolled her eyes, then made sure there was no goblin blood on the backs of her hands. It was hard enough showing up in town with gray-green skin and tusks that stuck out no matter how nicely you tried to smile. Add in some decorative blood splatters and the local humans would be lunging to grab their pitchforks and torches.

"The mayor asked us to clear the cave out on the way back," her father said. As the chieftain of their clan, Gorgo had the most dealings with the humans. He was much better at smiling nicely when they cowered.

Vola didn't say anything as she slung her ax across her back and trudged home. Their cottage wasn't far now, and as much as she loved her parents, there was only so much of them she could take. An entire weekend outdoors with constant reminders to keep her eyes open and her blade sharp had her on edge.

It wasn't that she didn't like beheading goblins. Oh sure, there were plenty who were peaceful and left the village alone, but these had been kidnapping baby sheep and stealing young maidens for their rituals. The mayor had already tried reasoning with them, but they'd just kept stealing and kidnapping. And sometimes it was nice to let off steam with some well-sanctioned blood shed.

But that was all the village saw them as. Exterminators. The orc clan that had settled on the outskirts of the village was tolerated as long as they kept the bandits away in the winter and stayed on their side of the street.

Yes, fine. Vola was good at bloodshed. Almost as good as her parents.

She just wanted to be good at other things as well.

Too bad no one saw the daughter of an orc chieftain and a human barbarian as anything other than a sword for hire.

"What's wrong?" Gorgo asked, catching up to her as she broke through the forest at the very edge of the village and stomped up the stairs to their cottage. Her mother's daylilies bobbed beside the door.

"Nothing," Vola said. "It's just…don't you ever get tired of swinging your sword for no reason?"

Gorgo blinked and opened the door. "There were a lot of dead goblins in that cave when we were done. That's plenty of reason."

"That's not what I mean," Vola mumbled.

"Boots off," Lydia said behind them. "Weapons by the door. If I have to scrub mud or blood out of my rugs, I'll be very put out."

Vola obediently hung up her weapons, chewing her lip between her tusks. "I just mean don't you ever want to do something more?"

Gorgo beamed and slung his arm around her shoulders. "Of course."

Some of the tension melted from her shoulders. "Really?"

"That just means it's time to find you a job. I'll talk to some of our old adventuring buddies and we'll get you set up as a mercenary. Plenty of gold to be had clearing out goblin caves and wargle nests."

Vola winced and pulled out from under his arm. "Not really what I was going for, Dad."

Lydia smacked Gorgo's arm. "Don't go pushing her into a career. She's only sixteen."

Vola retreated up the stairs to her attic room while her parents whispered not so subtly behind her.

"Well, how else do you explain this mood? Orcs need to get out and bash things now and then to feel normal."

"It's not the bashing. She just spent all weekend bashing, and it didn't help. She's a teenager. Let her figure herself out."

Gorgo sighed gustily, and Vola echoed him as she pushed through her door and shut it behind her, cutting off their voices. She didn't even glance at the bed or the comfy chair her father had built from rough branches and wargle fur. She went straight to the window and flung it open, then climbed up to sit on the sill with her feet dangling out.

From here she could see the town hall where the humans gathered to talk about whatever it was humans talked about. Vola wasn't sure. Lydia wasn't a great example of human normalcy being married to an orc chief. And the humans all screamed and ran whenever Vola tried to smile at them. Hardly a way to make friends and fit in.

Across the way on the orc side of town, she could just make out her Aunt Urag chasing a couple of children out of her yard with a broom. They squealed as she swatted them, and the end of her broom scorched the earth as it passed. Aunt Urag was pissed apparently. They must have trampled her nightshade.

Vola tilted her face up toward the sun. Really, her parents were both wrong. But she had no idea how to explain herself to them. She needed to do something. But mercenary work wasn't it. Fighting was fine—in fact, fighting was the one thing she was really good at—but it had to mean something.

But every time she got there in her head, she asked herself, "mean what?"

And she still couldn't come up with an answer.

The next morning, Vola passed a group of orcs raising a pole in the center of their encampment. Blood red streamers flowed from the top, drifting in the breeze.

She raised a hand to shield her face and ducked through old man Terrence's back yard before any of them could notice her. She'd forgotten it was the orcish New Year, a time to celebrate orc rage and all the other hardships that made them strong.

As the chieftain, her father attended all the High Holy Days, but he'd never insisted Vola and Lydia be *religious* about it all, and Vola wasn't about to start now.

Through a hedge of raspberry bushes and over the next fence Vola found herself on the human side of town, just across the street from the temple. The last bell chimed as she slipped into the back and joined the other students jostling for places on the benches.

The other human students.

A couple in the back gave her wide-eyed looks or sniffed like they smelled something rotten, but mostly she avoided the notice of the rest.

Until she tripped over the leg of a bench, sending it crashing to its side and dumping a row of students on the flagstones. They cried out and suddenly everyone was looking at her.

Vola took a deep breath, fighting the urge to flee or draw her blade. Her long adolescent limbs only seemed to want to cooperate when she was fighting.

"Sorry," she mumbled. Then she stooped to right the bench and picked up the other students one by one to set them back in their places, fast enough none of them could muster a protest.

She plopped herself on the bench against the back wall, hunching her shoulders so her bulk wasn't so noticeable.

A slim girl in the front tossed her long blond hair over her shoulder and leaned in toward her friends. "When do you think the monster will give up and run off into the woods where it belongs?"

The girls all giggled while Vola bristled. At least the other students mostly ignored Vola. When she wasn't knocking them over. But Ella and her nearly identical friends Ellen and Elsie were always looking for someone to torment. A green someone.

The door at the end of the long musty temple opened and a man in a long drab robe with his gray hair growing out of a tonsure stepped to the lectern at the front of the room.

The old priest's glare scoured the class and found Vola against the wall.

"Oh, you're back." His nasally voice was as sour as ever.

Vola raised her chin. He said the same thing every day, but it still hadn't driven her away.

"You know I'm not wasting my time on someone without the aptitude to appreciate my tutelage," he said. "You'll get no special help."

Vola ground her teeth, tusks rubbing her top lip raw. "I'm aware."

"She probably doesn't even know what 'tutelage' means," Ella whispered.

The old priest cleared his throat. "Ignore the distraction, please," he told the others. "And open your books to your last lesson."

Vola ground her teeth and spread the pages of her primer, ready to force herself through the lesson yet again.

The words swam before her eyes, twisting on the page until she couldn't discern the difference between them. Why did humans all write their p's and q's exactly the same anyway? And she didn't even want to think about b's and d's.

Vola had to concentrate on each letter one at a time to get them to stand still, but she would get them to stand still. Even without help.

Because the priest might be right about it being harder for Vola than for everyone else. But he wasn't right about it being a wasted effort.

And she was far more stubborn than some spindly human.

By the end of the day, her head hurt, but she'd made it through the whole page. Maybe she wouldn't bother showing up the next day. She was already teaching herself; why did she put herself through the torture of all the sidelong looks and snide comments, anyway?

Because she wanted them to see. She wanted them to see her trying harder than all the rest of them. Because maybe one day, that would make a difference.

The older boys all jostled to leave the temple first while Vola stood and collected her book and papers.

As she moved to the door, Ella pushed past with a huff.

"Really, Vola. I know you're huge, but you could at least try not to take up the entire doorway."

The girls laughed.

Red crept from the edges of Vola's vision and threatened to overwhelm the whole temple.

She closed her eyes and took a deep breath, forcing down the rage that belonged to the orc half of her. *Words*, she told herself. *Use words. That's what humans value.*

She was just forming an appropriate comeback when gasps and frantic shuffling filled the echoing space of the temple. Her eyes snapped open, and she found her classmates retreating to make room at the door.

A man in gold-washed steel armor strode down the center of the temple, the light from the high windows reflecting from his breastplate so Vola had to squint to get a good look at him. A sword hung from his hip. Jewels glinted from the cross-guard but the hilt was well used.

The warrior raised his helm and winked at the girls ogling from the sides. Ella swooned into a friend's arms.

With a start Vola realized the man had sharply pointed ears.

She'd heard of elves, but she'd never seen one before.

Vola waited for the priest to make some snide comment about non-humans in the temple but the old man fell over himself to greet the newcomer at the front of the temple.

"Welcome, paladin," he said, holding out his hands. "Welcome. What can I do for you? Are you here on a quest? Do you need accommodations? Refreshments?"

The elf flashed a grin. "A place to pray is all," he said. "Henri? Will you take care of the horses?"

Vola hadn't even noticed the other man who'd come into the temple in the paladin's shadow. His cropped gray hair and eclectic choice of leather and plate armor made him easily overlooked.

The second man, Henri, grinned and lifted his fingers to his forehead in a lazy salute. He turned to exit the temple, and over his shoulder, Vola caught sight of a gleaming white charger stamping its hoof in the stable yard.

The priest turned and saw the rest of them gawking near the door and hurried to shoo them away.

Vola went just as reluctantly as the others.

"Who is he?" she whispered without realizing she was going to say it out loud.

"A paladin," the priest answered, putting his hand on her shoulder and pushing when she took too long to leave.

"What's a paladin?"

"A white knight, a holy warrior chosen to protect the people who can't protect themselves," the priest said. "They spend their lives fighting evil." He glared at her. "Which means you should get out of here."

Vola's cheeks went tight and hot as he shut the door in her face. That word had plagued her all her life. It shouldn't bother her so much now. Especially coming from the priest who'd abused it so much it had lost its meaning.

But he'd just welcomed another non-human into the temple. He'd treated an elf with a reverence he only showed for old wine and soft cheese. She'd never heard him speak of anyone with such respect.

And Vola couldn't help but wonder which meant more. The fact that the man wasn't an orc? Or was it that he was a paladin?

Vola bit savagely into her sandwich letting loose bits of bread and barbecued wargle fall on her plate.

She had an idea floating around in the back of her head that she couldn't quite articulate yet. Something that poked and prodded at the discontent that had been boiling under her skin but didn't quite fix it. Not yet.

They spend their lives fighting evil. Which means you should get out of here.

Hmph. The priest wouldn't know evil if it bit him in the ass.

Not that that was new. It was just...she couldn't get the image of shiny armor and that white charger out of her head. But that little scrap of daydream was all wrapped up with his sibilant voice in her ear.

She growled as she took another bite.

Her mother came into the room and stopped short when she saw Vola at the table. "You're supposed to be in school."

"Yeah, I am," Vola said to her sandwich. But she was teaching herself anyway. What difference did it make if she did it here instead of there?

Lydia eyed her sidelong across the rough table. "Everything all right?"

"Don't want to talk about it," Vola muttered.

Lydia's lips thinned, and her eyes went crinkly around the corners like they did when she was worried. "You know it's not healthy to keep all that anger inside, right? Letting it out and facing it will make you stronger in the end."

Vola snorted. "That's what the orcs believe."

"You are half orc," Lydia said. "And I've lived with your father for long enough that I think they have the right of it."

"You're probably the only human who's ever thought orcs were right for worshiping the Obstacles."

Lydia opened her mouth to respond, but the cottage door

swung open, smashing into the weapon rack on the wall. Gorgo stood on the threshold.

Lydia's outraged cry died when she saw her husband's face. "What—?"

"Bandits," Gorgo said, reaching past the door to grab his greatsword. "Attacking the village."

Vola's chair banged behind her as her mother raced for the door.

"They're out of season." Lydia grabbed up her ax and followed Gorgo out into the street.

"You want to try telling them that?"

"I will," Lydia said with a huff. "With my weapon."

"Coming, honey?" Gorgo said over his shoulder.

Vola was already pulling her own ax from the wall. "Woohoo, another fun-filled family outing."

"That's the spirit." Gorgo laughed and raced down the dusty street, a few paces behind his wife.

Vola hurried after them and froze on the corner, all the sarcasm rushing from her in a flood, leaving her limbs heavy.

Human villagers fled to the safety of their homes while the orcs streamed toward trouble. But from the screams carrying across the thatched roofs and the smell of smoke in the air, this wasn't just a brief raid from a couple desperate thieves. This was a concerted assault planned and executed to deal the most amount of damage in the least amount of time.

Vola's grip tightened on her ax haft, and she stepped forward to follow Lydia and Gorgo who were already disappearing toward the trouble.

A lithe figure ran smack into her back, knocking her off balance. She stumbled and turned, catching the blonde girl around the elbows.

"Ella, what are you doing?" she snapped. "You're running the wrong way. Get inside."

Ella whimpered and tried to pull out of her grasp. "They're coming from the other side of the village. They've set fire to the temple with the priest still inside. Nowhere is safe."

Vola's breath came quicker. The attack on the orc side of town had been a feint, a ruse to draw the orcs away from the human village.

Vola thrust Ella toward their cottage. "Get inside," she said. "You'll be safer in there."

"Ew, but that's your house."

Vola slammed the door in her face, trying not to feel too happy about it.

Then she cracked her neck and raced for the human half of town.

At the corner where the bakery backed up to the pub, she found the mayor crouched between the walls of the two buildings, several other townsfolk with him.

Vola slid to a halt beside them and peered out into the street. Sure enough, several buildings were on fire, sending thick black smoke billowing into the afternoon sky, including the temple across the street.

"Where are they coming from?" Vola asked the mayor before he could open his mouth.

He had more presence of mind than Ella and gulped before he pointed a steady finger. "They've been smashing through the shops, taking what they can carry. They're in the bakery now."

"How many?"

"At least six here," the mayor said. He mopped his red forehead with his sleeve and grimaced at the streak of sweat and soot he left on the white cloth. "I don't know how many total."

Vola tapped the corner of the building. Six goblins weren't that much. They fought berserker style, and as long as you didn't let them get too close, they couldn't mob you. But six bandits were bad. And these had already proved they were smart.

She was starting to regret not grabbing her parents before rushing over here. They were on the wrong side of town completely.

Vola's thoughts raced. The fires flickered from a copper bottomed pot in the nearest window, reminding her of sun on gold plate.

"The paladin," she whispered. They needed the paladin. She stuck her head out again and scanned the streets, looking for shining armor and a white horse.

Nothing. But she did hear a quiet nicker from behind the inn beside them. Vola signaled the mayor to stay put and crept to the corner, heart in her throat.

Please let him be here. She wasn't even sure who she prayed to. Anyone who might listen she guessed.

The horse in the alley behind the inn wasn't white. It was brown and the man at its side was dressed in an eclectic mix of leather and plate armor.

Henri. The man who'd been with the paladin in the temple. He carefully and quietly lifted three children up to sit on his horse. Their pale faces had gone blank with shock.

Vola's breath left her lungs in a whoosh. "Hey," she said quietly so as not to startle him. "That paladin you came with. We need him."

Henri glanced at him. The glint of humor in his eye was gone, replaced by calm determination.

"He's on the other side of town. Where the fighting started."

Vola huffed and ran a hand through her hair. "That was a feint. The bandits drew away the orcs, and now they're attacking here."

"I know. I'm trying to get as many people out as I can. Then I'll get him back over here."

Vola's lips thinned. "That may be too late."

"The bandits set fire to the temple with the priest still inside," a woman beside the mayor said. "He'll be dead before anyone can help. The gods have abandoned us."

Vola chewed her lip between her tusks. Maybe the woman was right. The gods hadn't left anyone around to help these people. She stared down at her hands.

Then her fingers clenched.

"Sir," she said to paladin's companion. "Er, knight?" How did she address him?

The man smiled. "Just Henri. I train knights. I don't claim to be one."

But his armor was well cared for and showed signs of battle. Clearly he knew how to use the blade that hung at his hip and the round shield he carried on his back.

"Will you get these people to safety?" Her gesture took in the children he'd already loaded onto the horse and the group with the mayor.

"Of course," Henri said swiftly. "What will you be doing?"

Vola called over her shoulder as she stepped out onto the main street, "Guarding your back so you can get away."

The door of the bakery smashed open, and Vola didn't have time to check their progress. She rushed forward before the bandits had a chance to make it out into the street.

The first one she caught bottle-necked in the doorway, his arms full of bread. His laughter cut off with a gurgle as she slashed her ax across his throat.

The three bandits behind him froze in the shop's front room, staring down at the body. The first to react was a woman, her hair tied up in braids and a slash of green paint across her face.

She screamed and rushed Vola.

Vola planted her feet, leveled her ax, and ducked the woman's charge.

The bandit went tumbling over her back into the street. The next one went for a blow to her head, and she met his sword with a block, the blade biting deep into her ax haft. She grunted and heaved and even a half grown orc's strength was better than a spindly bandit's. He staggered back into his fellow and they both went down in a heap.

There was an intake of air, and Vola turned to catch the woman with the face paint lurching at her, club raised. Vola pulled her elbow up awkwardly, caught in the narrow doorway, and managed to take the blow on her forearm.

She cried out and stumbled back, dropping her weapon. She tripped over the two fallen bandits and smashed them flat against the rough floor boards with her weight.

Vola winced and scrabbled for her ax. It lay just out of reach. He mom was going to kill her for that mistake.

One of the fallen bandits pushed her legs aside and surged to his feet, the woman right behind him.

The woman raised her club.

Vola kicked the man's groin and he fell back with a cry. Right into the woman's blow. He went limp, his dead weight falling into her, and together they crashed through the front window.

The last bandit wriggled under Vola's legs, and she stretched to grab her ax. The bandit had barely freed himself from her weight when he looked up to catch Vola's blow descending.

"Oh, shi—"

Her ax silenced him.

Vola climbed to her feet, using the counter to help, and she leaned there, breathing hard.

Then she lurched to the door to check the two bandits in the street. The man lay still, unconscious or dead, Vola couldn't tell. But the woman struggled under his weight, growling under her breath.

Vola didn't wait for her to free herself. She planted a solid kick in the woman's temple and watched her go limp.

Then she braced her hands on her knees and stared around the empty street.

She'd been lucky—so, so lucky—that she'd caught these by surprise. But the mayor had said there were at least six. So where were the other two?

The shops along the streets stood quiet except for the flames licking at their roofs. Broken glass strewn across the street reflected the fires, but there was no movement in any of the empty windows.

A raised voice came from the open door of the temple. Vola glanced at the roof, holding her breath. The flames licked up the sides, but the structure was much bigger and had been built much sturdier than the rest of the village. Vola hoped it would hold.

She stalked forward. Her wounded arm ached and sweat ran into her eyes and burned. At the door of the temple, she stopped and swiped her dirty sleeve across her face before she peered around the edge.

No one lurked in the main temple where they held lessons and services, but smoke wafted through the rafters.

Vola held her arm over her nose and ducked inside, avoiding the benches. Behind the main sanctuary, a door opened onto the priest's private rooms. Vola put her back to the wall and listened.

"—last time. Where's your treasure, old man?" a woman asked.

"I have no treasure," the priest answered, his voice gone hoarse from coughing or screaming. "I'm here to serve the gods."

"All temples have treasure. Altar ornaments, gold offerings."

"We're a small village—Ahh!"

Vola's teeth clenched at the sound of his scream. The priest might have made her life miserable, and a very, very small part of her felt vindicated by his pain, but the rest of her squirmed with it.

She took a deep breath and stepped around the doorframe.

Three bandits, not two—the mayor needed to go back to school for a bit—stood with their backs to the door. The priest lay across the floor, blood trickling from his neck. The lead bandit, a woman with more green paint, pressed her spiked mace against the wound.

The priest's eyes went wide as Vola slipped through the door, ax in hand.

"M-monster," he cried.

The woman rolled her eyes. "You don't think we're falling for that one, do you—"

Vola swung and the lead bandit fell under her ax. Surprise was the best ally, her dad always said. Take out the leader first, her mother would tell her. There's a good chance the rest might scatter if their head's been cut off.

The other two bandits jumped and stared at Vola, and she paused to see if they were the type to run or fight.

The nearest looked at her face then looked down at the bandit leader. Then he lunged at her.

Fight it was, then. Vola raised her ax and blocked his first blow. Then she ducked around the priest's desk and shoved. The solid piece of wood struck the man in the gut, and he doubled over gasping.

The second bandit threw himself across her back, and Vola staggered. His arm closed around her throat, cutting off her air.

She choked and coughed, her vision going dim. *Think, think, think.* Her parents would never forgive her for dying to two measly bandit.

With a heave, she slammed her attacker into the wall, once, twice, three times until she finally heard a crack and his grip loosened.

She shook the bandit's limp form off her back, and he slumped to the ground, blood running from his cracked skull.

Her last enemy growled and started around the desk.

Red tinged the edges of her vision, and Vola knelt to grasp the bottom of the priest's desk. She flipped the heavy piece of furniture into the bandit.

He collapsed between it and the wall.

Vola coughed, trying to draw a decent breath in the smoke filled room. She stumbled to the priest.

"Let's go," she said, stooping to grab him under the arms.

He pushed feebly at her hands. "Leave me," he said, closing his eyes. "I go to be with my gods now."

She squinted in the flickering light. Nothing seemed to be wrong with him except for some bruises and the stab on his collarbone.

"You'll be fine," Vola said. A creak from the ceiling above made her wince. "As long as we get out before the roof collapses."

He cracked an eye to glare at her. "If my gods wanted me to live, they would save me."

"They sent me to save you, you dingbat," she cried.

He spat. "An agent of the Obstacles? Never."

Vola ground her teeth. He would rather die than be rescued by an orc.

Well, she wouldn't give him the satisfaction.

She hauled his dead weight over her shoulder and climbed to her feet. His moans and litany of whining buzzed in her ears as she limped through the temple proper and out the door.

She gasped in the clear air outside and stumbled the last few feet to the temple yard gate. Then she dumped the priest unceremoniously in the street.

"Vola!" Her mother's voice cut through the priest's complaining, and cool hands smoothed the soot from her face. "Are you all right?"

Vola coughed once more and raised her burning eyes to gaze at the villagers gathered in the street. Henri stood at the temple fence, squinting up at the roof.

"What happened?" she croaked. "They were supposed to get out."

"We've swept the town and driven the rest of the bandits out," Lydia said. "The paladin and your father are setting up patrols to make sure they're well and truly gone. But the mayor said you'd gone into the temple and hadn't come out."

"Dishonoring my death," the priest moaned.

Lydia glared down at him.

"Don't mind him," Henri said, turning so the flickering flames lit up the scar that pulled from the corner of his eye all the way down his cheek. "You did good and deserve all the thanks he's not giving you."

"I didn't do it for the thanks," Vola said before she'd realized it was true.

Henri tilted his head. "Then why?"

Vola surveyed the villagers standing in the street. The mayor seemed unscathed and aside from his moaning, the priest was alive and well, too.

A surge of pride made her chest swell, and she was surprised to find that the priest's words didn't actually matter. Who cared if he would rather die than be saved by a "monster?"

"I did it because it was the right thing to do." She'd saved them because they couldn't save themselves, but she could.

For the first time in a long time, the itch behind her breastbone that urged her on and scratched at her until she didn't know whether to run or fight died down.

She knew how to fight. But now she knew why she wanted to fight. She could spend her life fighting evil, because it was the right thing to do. But also so that one day people like the priest would look at her and see more than a monster.

TWO

VOLA USED her wooden practice shield to lock up her opponent's weapon, then spun so the winter sunlight shining across the training yard blinded him.

But the paladin trainee didn't need to see her to crowd into her, lips spread wide in a sneer.

"Go home, monster," he hissed.

Her eyes narrowed, but she kept her head. The old priest had more venom in his little toe than this boy did in his entire being. She grunted and used her shield to dump him on his butt in the dirt.

The trainee swiped sweaty blond hair out of his eyes in order to glare up at her.

"Get out of the ring, Geston," one of the knight trainers called from behind the fence. "You let her beat you, now get over it. Do better next time."

The trainee, Geston, climbed to his feet and spit. Vola didn't bother stepping back. She'd had four years to get used to the other trainees and all the ways they could make her life miserable.

They weren't the ones that mattered. They gathered at the

edges of the fence, churning the slush into mud in order to grumble any time she won a practice bout.

The knight trainers didn't matter either, in the end, even if they were the ones to mark down her progress.

No one mattered except the Paladin Council and the gods. They were the ones who would decide her fate. Everyone else was just window dressing.

Vola moved to the edge of the ring, the sun beating on her head even though the air was cool with winter's chill. The mud of the practice ring would freeze into solid ruts tonight after dark. She made a mental note to watch her feet during training tomorrow. The week of vigils would be a hell of a time to break an ankle.

A few men gathered behind the boys at the railing. They turned their backs as Vola climbed over and returned her practice gear to the racks. Some were trainers, some were full knights here to choose a candidate to mentor. None would look her in the face without a smirk or a snub. Even though after four years of training she'd grown into her limbs, and now she was the strongest trainee at the Whiteshield Academy.

She swiped her towel from the fence and wiped her face and neck before making her way through the throng to the building that held the Knight Commander's offices.

The yard was packed this time of day. Most of the trainers reserved the mornings for classwork and the afternoons for practice and drills. So Vola had to duck around several groups of students. The ones in her year turned their shoulders and closed ranks. As if she didn't already know she wasn't welcome with them.

Some of the younger ones waved a greeting before being shushed by their peers. She'd made a few friends among them, giving some extra fighting lessons. But they'd learn soon enough not to address her in public. Not if they wanted the respect of the Paladin Council.

A low rumble started beside the door to the council offices, as the rest of her year-mates gathered near the board on the wall. Vola stopped at the edge of the crowd and lifted her chin. She was tall enough to see the little scraps of paper that hung there, left-overs from previous announcements. But there wasn't a list. Not yet at least.

Her heart hammered in her chest. She hadn't missed the vigil assignments, but that didn't keep her mouth from going dry.

After four years of trainee status, the vigil was the only thing separating her from becoming a true paladin candidate. All the classes on tactics and monster types and fighting styles, all the training in the ring, and all the snubs and insults from the trainers and her year-mates would be worth it after this week.

As long as one of the gods found her worthy enough.

She shook her head. That was what the vigil was for. A trainee stood vigil in the chapel all night to acquaint themselves with the gods they might serve. And in the morning, if one of those gods had chosen them—and a knight master agreed to mentor them—then they were considered an actual candidate who could earn their shield.

That last bit, that was the important thing. Because the last few years of training happened outside of the academy. Under the direction of a knight master.

If her vigil went well, if a god chose her and a knight master picked her, then she could leave this place forever. Finally.

And Knight Commander Imralen wouldn't be able to do anything about it.

A squirrely looking man with prominent teeth and a pair of dirty spectacles sliding down his nose pushed through the door.

The Knight Commander's toady. In four years Vola had never learned his name because even the Knight Commander had never used it. The man had inserted himself so firmly into Imralen's shadow, that was all he was ever remembered for.

The man frowned at the crowd of trainees and pushed his spectacles up his nose before he turned and nailed a list to the board beside the door.

The trainees surged forward.

Vola held her ground, her breath coming faster.

She let the surge of the crowd part around her before deliberately stepping out and clearing a way for herself. Her bulk alone made the others step back so she could peer at the list. The letters twitched and tried to scramble off the page, but she concentrated, running her eyes down the names, looking for her own.

Volagra. Volagra.

It wasn't there.

She started again from the top. Letters always squiggled and refused to hold still. Maybe her name had just gotten lost for a second. She didn't have to panic. Yet.

Geston and a couple of his friends stepped up beside her, found their names immediately, and turned to sneer at her.

"Looks like the Knight Commander agrees with us," he said. "You'll have to go home, monster."

They guffawed and left Vola standing in front of the board, staring at a list that didn't have her name on it.

Her fists clenched, nails digging into her palms hard enough to draw blood as the rest of the trainees trickled away, whispering about their vigils.

Her name wasn't on the list. She hadn't been assigned a vigil. Without a vigil she couldn't be chosen by a god. Without a god she wouldn't get a mentor. And without a mentor she would never earn her shield.

Four years wasted. Four years of taunts and back-breaking work.

Vola straightened her spine. No.

She'd had to fight her way in here in the first place. She'd had to fight every day to stay. This was no different. If Knight Commander Imralen thought she was going to run home just because her name wasn't on some stupid list, he clearly hadn't been paying attention.

She strode for the door to the offices.

The squirrely man held up a hand to stop her. "Trainees aren't allowed in today."

"Screw that." She picked him up and set him down out of her way.

Her boots made a satisfying thump as she stomped up the steps to Knight Commander Imralen's office.

Vola didn't bother knocking.

The door struck the wall as she slammed through, making the tall gray-haired man at the desk beyond jump. His flint hard eyes narrowed, and his jaw clenched.

"Volagra," Knight Commander Imralen said.

She made a concerted effort to unclench her teeth and speak. "I wasn't assigned a vigil." As if he didn't know.

He raised an unimpressed eyebrow and went back to his paperwork. "You're not ready."

"Not ready?" Vola said. She threw out an arm to indicate the rest of the academy. "Every trainee in my year got an assignment except me. How am I any less ready than them?"

"Every now and then we have a student who doesn't keep up with the rest of their peers. You just happened to be the one for this year."

She poked her finger at his paperwork, forcing him to look up at her. "I'm the best damn trainee you have, and you know it."

The lines around his mouth deepened as he stared at her offending finger. "And yet, I've decided you're not ready to be a candidate."

"Give me a reason," she said. "Just one."

He steepled his hands in front of him. "You want a reason? Fine. I cannot allow your evil to taint this academy, Volagra."

She drew back, brows lowering. "What evil?" she said quietly. Though she could guess. It was the same reason mothers pulled their children away from her on the street. The same reason men with torches and pitchforks drove orc families away from their neighborhoods.

"Orcs worship the Obstacles," Imralen said, casually straightening his papers. "Paladins only ever represent the Virtues."

She shut her teeth tight on the flood of arguments that she wanted to use. The Obstacles weren't evil. They just represented the darker side of human existence. Things like rage and shame and jealousy. And orcs revered them because overcoming hardship was the fastest way to become strong. Nothing about any of that made orcs evil.

But Imralen knew all that.

"I haven't worshiped an Obstacle even once in my life," Vola said through gritted teeth. And attending the occasional High Holy day with her parents hardly counted. Everyone did that.

"Nevertheless, I can't allow you to set foot in that chapel and risk the possibility of an Obstacle choosing you."

"Obstacles don't choose paladins."

"And if that's true, then you can wait until I'm certain you are virtuous enough that you won't taint our chapel or our academy."

He waved her out and then bent back over his papers, dismissing her before she was even gone.

Vola stood there, swallowing over and over again, the red beating at the edge of her vision a direct contradiction to the calm she struggled to exude.

Imralen didn't mean a word of what he said. He didn't actually believe an Obstacle would choose her. He just didn't want an orc graduating from his academy. And he could say she wasn't ready over and over and over again until she gave up and went home.

Or she snapped and proved his words right.

She cracked her neck and fought down a pleasant daydream of leaping across the table and wrapping her hands around his neck. It might be pleasant but the paperwork would be the real murder.

Though the snapping thing was still a possibility. She couldn't stay here another month let alone another year or ten, trying to prove herself to men who'd already made up their minds about her.

But she also wasn't going home. Now that she knew what she wanted to be—what she was *supposed* to be—she would not retreat. She would not settle for something less than knighthood.

Imralen might have been stubborn. But Vola was half orcish. Her mother had often said her head was thicker than a stone wall and twice as hard to tumble.

She wouldn't let him beat her.

Imralen glanced up at her. "Did I not make myself clear, trainee? What are you still doing here?"

She didn't give him the respect of an answer. She just turned on her heel and left the offices.

Imralen didn't dictate her future. She refused to leave her life in the hands of a man who saw her as nothing more than a beast to be humiliated and broken. There was only one authority she needed to become a paladin.

Time to see if the gods agreed with the Knight Commander or with Vola.

The vigils for the current batch of trainees were supposed to start the next evening. So Vola didn't have long to make this work.

As soon as the sun went down and the training yard cleared, Vola crept out of the dormitories and made her way to the chapel on the other side of the yard. It should be deserted this time of night.

She wore a simple linen shirt and a pair of loose pants, and the chill winter air cut right through them, but nothing touched the fire burning under her skin. She was getting out of here. She was finally taking her future into her own hands, and as long as everything went right, she'd be riding away from this place in the morning.

As long as the gods didn't agree with Imralen.

She wouldn't think about that possibility.

A lone trainee wandered across the dark yard and stopped to take a swig of something contraband he'd secreted in his coat. Vola pressed herself into the shadows of the wall, waiting for him to move on.

Finally he staggered to the threshold of the dormitory, and Vola was free to move toward the chapel again. She darted to the big carved doors and reached for the handle.

Locked.

Dammit. Who kept a chapel locked at all times? What if someone wanted to pray in the middle of the night?

Or sneak in to hold an unsanctioned vigil?

Vola chewed her lip and stared up at the imposing facade. She'd always figured that if she was going to talk to a god it would be better outdoors where she could see the sky and feel the wind. But tradition was set in stone around here, so she wasn't about to mess with the vigil ritual. And vigils were held in the chapel.

Well, if Imralen couldn't stop her, a measly little locked door was nothing. She slipped around the edges of the building checking for windows.

The ones along the sides were all tall and stained glass. Not only would she feel bad about breaking them, the noise would bring every paladin and paladin trainee in the academy.

Imralen would have no trouble throwing her out, then. The only reason he hadn't yet was because she'd been very, very careful not to break any rules. You know, besides the unspoken one about being an evil orc.

She turned the corner to the back of the chapel. There. A normal looking window was set high over the back door the priests used. She might even fit through it.

She just had to figure out how to get up there.

If she remembered correctly, there were some moldy crates hanging out by the stables this morning.

She tiptoed to the outbuilding, avoiding the hostlers who played cards around the wood stove, and grabbed a couple crates. She could fit four of them under her arms as she huffed back to the chapel. There were some advantages to being tall.

Vola stacked the crates, eying the window to line them up.

They wobbled precariously as she settled her weight on them. She grabbed the sill to steady herself and tried the window.

It was locked, too. Dammit. Maybe the gods really didn't want her to be a paladin.

She squinted, trying to see the latch inside.

The crate under her feet creaked. That was all the warning she had before the moldering wood gave way, and she crashed through to the ground.

She stumbled out of the debris and landed on her butt in the dirt. A grunt escaped between her lips, but she managed to stifle the rest of her cry.

That had hurt more than any paladin trainee would be willing to admit. She rolled to her side to survey the wreckage. Bits of rotten wood littered the ground, but at least none of the splinters were in her butt. That would have been hard to explain in the morning.

Nothing stirred the still air, so her dramatic fall hadn't woken the entire academy. A small blessing but one she'd grab with both hands.

She grimaced and climbed to her feet, cracked her back, and then glared up at the window.

"It certainly is up there," a voice said.

Vola jumped and whipped around.

A man lounged against the corner of the chapel, arms crossed over his chest. He wore an eclectic mix of plate and leather armor, well used and well taken care of. The moonlight illuminated his steel gray hair and glinted from the scar that pulled at the corner of his eye and traveled down his neck.

He grinned at her, wide and friendly.

She blew out her breath, relaxing just a little. Of all the people to have caught her, Henri was by far her best prospect.

The old trainer wasn't at the academy all that often—usually he was off with a paladin candidate, helping them earn their shield, like the elf he'd worked with in Vola's village. But he showed up every now and then and always went out of his way to treat Vola like any other trainee.

She specifically remembered him bent over a book of tactics, explaining the troop movements to a frustrated young woman who couldn't make the words sit still long enough to read them.

She'd gotten a lot of grief for that one. All the trainees spoke about him in hushed tones and they all hoped to be his next candidate. Clearly he was too good to be helping an orc. Even if he wasn't a full knight.

"I, uh, don't know what you mean," Vola said, eyes flicking to the window.

Henri's grin grew broader. "Then I guess you'd better try harder. Or smarter."

He pushed himself off the wall with a wink and then disappeared around the corner of the chapel.

Leaving a ladder propped where he'd been standing.

That definitely hadn't been there before.

Vola gulped and peered around the corner, trying to catch a glimpse of Henri. But he was gone already. The yard stood clear and empty.

No one to see her. And a convenient ladder where there hadn't been one before.

Was this a trick? A trap to get her to thrown out?

If it was Imralen or any of the paladin council, she'd believe it in a heartbeat. But Henri was different.

Every candidate he'd ever trained had gone on to become paragons of justice and mercy. Holy warriors dedicated to the good of the world.

Vola blew out her breath. She could either believe he had good intentions and seize her chance to get out of here. Or she could second guess everything until the sun rose and she was truly stuck.

Her choice.

She grabbed the ladder and dragged it into place.

The window would still be locked. But maybe once she got up there, she'd be able to jiggle it open. The shutters in the dormitories were cheap enough that if you leaned on them the right way they popped open. A trick many tardy trainees had used in their time here.

The window swung open at her touch.

A shiver went down Vola's spine. She'd checked it. She *had*, she knew she had.

She shook her head. Maybe it had just been stuck before.

The frame squeezed her sides as she shimmied through and dropped to the floor inside. None of the acolytes actually slept here since the chapel was really only used for vigils and High Holy days, so the back rooms were just for storage and stood empty tonight.

A lone candle burned in the main sanctuary, sending flickering shadows up to the faces of the gods painted on the back wall. A massive mural stretched from one side of the chapel to the other, depicting every Greater Virtue as benevolent giants with hundreds of Lesser Virtues gathered at their feet.

The only ones missing from this pantheon were the Obstacles.

Vola gazed up at the shadowed faces of the Greater Virtues. Maxim and Ona looked especially unforgiving in the wavering light. And they were the two who chose the most paladins. The Greater Virtue of Strength and Loyalty and the Greater Virtue of Honor.

Vola gulped. She was here. She'd made it inside. Now she just needed to sit her vigil.

The older candidates had described it as a night of contemplation and prayer. Of supplication to the gods you were about to serve.

Vola had never been much for praying. Orcs in general didn't really like to ask for help. It defeated the purpose of suffering and hardship if you asked for help getting out of it. And Vola's parents had always been so competent. They'd taught her to be competent, too.

But knights were supposed to be humble as well as strong. Their power didn't come from inside themselves. It came from the god who'd chosen them. And Vola desperately needed a god to choose her.

It wouldn't be too hard to pray for that. She'd been wishing and hoping for it for four years. And praying was only a step away from hoping.

She knelt.

A clinking from the front step of the chapel startled Vola from her reverie. She blinked, her neck stiff and her knees numb from kneeling on the stone floor. Light came pouring through the tall windows lining the chapel.

How had she missed the sun rising?

Something jingled, like a ring of keys dropped on the threshold outside.

"Just open the door." Imralen's voice cut through the thick doors, like an ax through a board.

"I'm sorry, Knight Commander. We never usually lock it."

"Yes, well, I didn't want any vermin infesting the place the night before we begin the vigils."

Vola staggered to her feet, heart in her throat. This was it. If she was going to become a paladin this was the moment the gods had to choose her. There was no more waiting. If Imralen dragged her out of here, they would have lost their chance.

She craned her neck to look up at the Greater Virtues. How did this work? None of the paladin candidates had ever said. They told the younger trainees that the moment was secret and sacred between them and their god. She'd always assumed it would become obvious once she'd gotten here.

A key clicked in the latch behind her. The bell toll that said her time was running out.

She closed her eyes. "Please," she said. Everything she'd had to say she'd said during the night. She'd poured out her arguments into the still wintry air. She'd laid out the logic of choosing her. She'd even revealed the deepest desires in her heart. The will that drove her to be better and stronger than the ones who doubted her. Who doubted all orcs.

"Please," she said again as the hinges creaked.

Nothing. The gods stood silent above her, their painted faces flat and expressionless in the bright morning light. As disapproving and uncaring as everyone who'd ever looked at Vola and said "no."

She was on her own the same way she'd been for the last four years.

"Volagra." Imralen's voice cracked across the empty space.

She flinched, her teeth grinding hard enough to creak. It was the hardest thing she'd ever done to turn and face the ending of her dream. There was no way Imralen would let her stay now.

The Knight Commander stood just inside the chapel, his mouth thin and white and his eyes hard as he stared at her. An acolyte shifted his feet beside him, hands playing nervously with the ring of keys. Several members of the paladin council including Imralen's toady crowded behind him.

"Commander," Vola said, voice grating. Her breath puffed in the cold air. She didn't say anything more. If he was going to kick her out, she was going to make him work for it.

"How dare you violate the sanctity of our chapel—"

"I haven't violated anything. I was praying. Standing vigil. That's what it's for, right?"

"I did not give you permission."

"No, you didn't. I've earned the right to try so I had to take it when you wouldn't give it to me."

Imralen strode to the center of the sanctuary which left the door clear enough for the rest of the council to shuffle in. Behind them, several of the knight masters crowded and trainees peered over their shoulders to see what was going on.

Vola straightened her shoulders.

"You do not belong there," Imralen said through his teeth.

"I've spent four years proving I belong just as much as anybody else. All I wanted was the chance to try."

His expression smoothed, and his eyes traveled up to the mural behind her. "Fine. You've tried. Was your vigil successful?"

He dropped his gaze to hers as she went hot and then cold all over. The blood pounded in her ears. She could argue forever that she deserved the right to stand here, but it wouldn't change the fact that the day had dawned and she stood here alone.

Vola opened her mouth just as a breeze touched her cheek. It took her a moment to realize why that sent a shiver down her spine.

The breath of air hadn't come from the door.

It had come from the mural at her back.

Imralen's eyes went wide as a light grew behind Vola, sending her jagged shadow stretching across the floor. The air changed as if someone stood behind her shoulder.

A hand clasped her shoulder, making Vola draw in a sharp breath. She wanted to turn, to see who stood there, but she was afraid to break the moment. She was afraid if she turned the hand would drop and she'd face empty air again.

"Not alone," a voice said out of the gentle breeze. Right into her ear as if it was meant only for her. "Not empty air."

The voice rose, a shush of wind and the shing of a blade being drawn. "Hello, Imralen."

Imralen jerked. "You," he said. "You choose her?"

"I do."

He barked a laugh. "That's fitting."

Who exactly was standing with her? Vola fought the urge to shrug, not willing to disconnect herself from the presence behind her. A god was a god. It didn't matter who had chosen her as long as she was chosen.

"Laugh again and you'll discover why I'm called the lady of sharp implements," the voice said.

Imralen made a cursory effort to wipe the smile from his face. It didn't quite work. He still smirked as he said. "Yes, my lady."

"Carry on, Vola," the voice said in her ear, and Vola got the impression she was the only one who could hear it again. "You have much work to do. But I know you are up to the task."

"Yes, my lady," Vola whispered, keeping her voice much more respectful than Imralen's had been.

The presence behind her shoulder faded, and the light dimmed until her shadow spread evenly from the morning sun.

The hand lingered a moment longer, and Vola tried to memorize the feel of it, the weight of it on her skin.

Gods had always been so abstract to Vola. Virtues and Obstacles alike. None had ever felt so real or complicated, like a sister calling to her from just over her shoulder.

She looked up at Imralen, a fierce grin making her cheeks ache. "You have to make me a candidate, now," she said.

His smirk remained in place, souring her pleasure. "Of course," he said. "As soon as you have a mentor. You might have a god, but you need an earthly knight to train you until you earn your shield."

He threw out his hand, indicating the knights gathered in the doorway.

"Will any of them agree to train an orc with a laughingstock of a goddess?"

Vola's gaze swept the array of figures. It was just one step. A small one, too. She'd already convinced one of the pantheon to take her on. Surely there had to be one mortal in the entire world who believed an orc could be a paladin.

As she looked over them, the knight masters shuffled their feet. None of them met her eyes. Some of them found their fingernails fascinating, others glared at her feet. None of them spoke up.

One face in the crowd actually looked at her.

Henri lounged against the wall beside the door, eyes on her. His grin twitched as if to say "let's make some mischief."

"I'll take her," he said loud enough to carry across the chapel.

Imralen started and spun around. His eyes narrowed on Henri. "You aren't a knight."

"You've never made that distinction before. No, I'm not a

knight. I'm better than a knight. I train knights. I train the best damn knights who come out of this academy." He tilted his head. "And you know it or you wouldn't let me ride away with them every year."

"I have plenty more promising trainees I was saving for you to look at—"

"I like Volagra," Henri said. "I'll take her."

"You can't—"

"I said, I'll take her." Henri's chin raised as his voice went firm and final.

Imralen's lips stretched thin over his teeth. His nostrils flared, and Vola waited for him to dash her last chance. He could order Henri to stand down, to take someone else. The old trainer would ride away with another candidate, and Vola would be alone again.

Imralen swallowed. "Fine, Trainer Henri."

Vola bit her lip on any noise she could have made. Knight Commander Imralen was caving? Gods, she'd never seen such a thing.

"I can see my words won't dissuade you," Imralen said through his teeth. "But know this. Her evil will break through eventually. One day it will crack that facade of good she's fooled you with and it will be your downfall."

"You're right," Henri said, hands in his pockets. "Your words mean very little to me."

Imralen's lips twisted. He cast one more poisonous glance at Vola and swept out of the chapel. The rest of the paladin council scrambled to follow.

Henri stepped across the flagstones to Vola as the others all trickled out into the yard.

He cocked his head up at her. She was taller than him by a good four inches.

She looked down at this man who would train her and travel with her for the years it took to earn her shield. He didn't look like much in his mismatched armor with his face seamed by weather and scarring. But he'd trained the best knights in Southglen. And he'd faced down the paladin council for her.

"So do you want to rest today? Or do you want to get out of here immediately?" He cast her a sidelong look like he already knew the answer.

"I want to get out," she said. It wasn't like she had anyone to say goodbye to. And she looked forward to the next phase of her life, following this man with the easy grin.

"I don't blame you," he said, turning for the door.

Vola stepped to follow him and an unfamiliar weight clunked against her chest.

She glanced down. A pendant hung from a silver chain, dangling over her heart. A long hooked fish knife. The symbol for Cleavah, Lesser Virtue and goddess of Vengeful Housewives.

Vola spun to search the mural. All the Lesser Virtues crowded at the feet of the Greater Virtues. It was nearly impossible to make them out individually. But near the bottom right, Vola thought she saw a hand clenched around the handle of a fish knife.

Imralen had called her goddess a laughingstock. But at least she had one now. Her hand curled around the pendant. It was her emblem. Her connection to the goddess. It would allow her to contact Cleavah and Cleavah to work through her.

Never alone, she'd said. Not anymore.

Vola turned to follow Henri.

He waited on the threshold of the chapel, a sheathed sword across his palms. "It's tradition. When a knight master takes on a candidate he gives them a sword. To signify they are ready to use their strength to serve. I'm not a knight, but you're definitely a candidate."

Vola took the blade from him, her fingers sliding across the worn leather sheath. It didn't look like much. But it was more about what it meant. She'd always used hand me down axes from her mother, but this settled into her hand like a long lost memory.

"Thank you," she said, meaning so much more than just those two words.

"You'll need a name," Henri said, tilting his face up toward the sun.

She cocked her head. "What?"

"A paladin name. You choose one when you leave the academy to earn your shield."

Vola turned her face up to the sun as well. It warmed her despite the winter air. Leaving the academy with Henri at her side and Cleavah at her back felt like stepping out of a dark cave into the morning light. Out of loneliness into the company of two people who believed in her.

But she didn't just want to be the one stepping into the light. She wanted to be the torch. No, even that was too small. She wanted to be the blazing sun.

"Lightbringer," she said. "I want to be Lightbringer."

PART TWO
SORREL

Sorrel's origin story is best read after *Death and Devotion.*

THREE

Sorrel Thornbough sat on the edge of her seat in the monastery library, listening to Father Naemon's soothing baritone relate the strictures of Maxim. Beside her, Tallah had drifted off, chin propped on her hand. Brother Ferell, who was supposed to be keeping the novices awake, snored in the corner.

Father Naemon, who might have been going a little deaf, didn't notice.

Sorrel fought to keep her eyes open, kicking her short legs over the edge of the over-sized chair. The abbot's voice was as soothing as a hot bath, and he tended to drone like the bees that lived in the hives behind the refectory. It would have been way easier to pay attention if today's lesson had been about Jodin Battlecalled. Hero of the Endless War and founder of their order.

Sorrel let her gaze wander as she pictured the hero swinging Maxim's Warhammer through hoards of enemies.

Another voice carried through the window, making her sit up. This one could never drone. It was dry and sharp and called out the practice forms so that everyone in the monastery could hear, let alone his students.

Sorrel glanced at Father Naemon, who didn't look up from the lectern, then she slipped off her chair and stood on her tiptoes to see out the window.

Master Bao stood in the courtyard with fifteen monks, all following his instruction.

A slow smile spread across Sorrel's face.

Father Naemon coughed, and the other novices sat up, pretending they'd been attentive all along. But he still didn't look up.

Sorrel crept toward the stairs that led down to the refectory and the kitchens.

"Psst," Tallah hissed behind her.

Sorrel cast a glare over her shoulder at the older novice.

Tallah's feet didn't quite reach the floor either, but she kept them rigid and still. "You're going to get into trouble."

Sorrel rolled her eyes. Trouble was always worth it as long as it was the fun sort of trouble.

Father Naemon resumed his lesson, coming close to drowning out Master Bao's voice, and Sorrel gave Tallah a jaunty wave.

Tallah just sniffed as Sorrel disappeared down the steps. At the bottom she slowed, then darted across the refectory to the kitchen where Brother Gregor reigned.

A blast of warm yeasty air hit her, and she crept along the edge of the kitchen avoiding Brother Gregor's massive feet as the cook swung a sizzling pan overhead and headed for the big fireplace against the far wall.

Sorrel easily ducked under a wooden table. She didn't even have to bow her head. The four year old halfling barely came up to a human's knees.

"I see you under there," Brother Gregor said.

Sorrel popped her head out with a pout. "How?"

The monk snorted. "You may be small but you're not that

sneaky. Keep your feet low when you walk. And get some new sandals. Those flap."

The halfling stared at her feet. The sandals were built for a human child and stuck out two inches past her toes. "Thanks," she said and slipped out from under the other end of the table and scampered for the door.

"Master Bao still won't let you join his class," the cook called, grabbing a salt shaker as big as his hand. "He's made it clear."

"We'll see," Sorrel said over her shoulder as she pushed out the door. It was what the adults always said when they didn't want to talk about something anymore.

The door let out to the courtyard. The dormitories and the chapel formed the other two sides of a square across from the kitchen and refectory and the sun was high enough to shine directly down into the open space.

Sorrel passed a statue of Maxim, the Greater Virtue of Strength and Loyalty, and she hopped up to slap the god's toe where it rested on its plinth. For luck.

In the center of the courtyard, a bald monk as dark as freshly tilled spring soil with a long white beard braided down his front led his fifteen students in a breathing exercise.

"Breathe in with strength. And out with loyalty," he said. He raised both arms like a stork and slowly brought his left foot to his right knee. Then held the position.

Sorrel slipped along the back wall, keeping her feet low like Brother Gregor had said, making sure her sandals didn't flap. She found a good spot where she could peer between two gray-clad monks. Then she raised her arms just like Master Bao.

Another short figure to her right gave her a sidelong look and a grin. Sorrel's best friend, Hazel. They'd grown up together and the dwarf had always been Sorrel's favorite. Probably because she was nearly as short as Sorrel. She'd only just been allowed to join Master Bao's class.

A few of the other monks wobbled on one foot, but Sorrel kept her balance and focused on breathing in and out, concentrating on the sound of Master Bao's voice.

"Breathe in with strength," he said again, voice calm but carrying across the courtyard. "Breathe out with loyalty. Only when you are centered can you strike with the might of Maxim."

His left hand curled beside his chest and his right struck out, punching the air in front of him.

The monks followed suit. Two fell over.

"Center yourself," Master Bao said. "Your feet must always be planted on Maxim's truths. Then you can strike from any unstable ground."

The two who'd fallen scrambled to their feet, faces red.

"Try again." Master Bao breathed in deep. "Sorrel."

Sorrel flinched. Still balancing on one foot with her fist out, she leaned far enough over to peer around the monk in front of her and meet Master Bao's direct gaze.

He raised an eyebrow. "What are you doing?"

She looked down at herself and then back up at him. "Practicing."

"I did not give you permission."

She stuck her lower lip out and shook her head.

"Go back to your lessons, little one," Master Bao said, turning away. "Father Naemon will be wondering where you are."

Sorrel dropped her foot to the ground and scampered down the line of monks. "I want to fight. I want to learn."

"You are too small."

"That's a good thing. I don't hit the ground as hard." She glanced at the two monks who'd wobbled.

Master Bao's lips twitched like he suppressed a smile, and Sorrel sensed an opening. "Please, Master Bao. Please."

"You do not have the discipline, yet," he said. "To follow

through with training. I cannot trust that you will show up day after day. It requires dedication. Not a passing interest."

Sorrel's lips tightened, and she planted her hands on her hips. "You let Hazel be here."

Master Bao's gaze flicked to the little dwarf towards the back with the bushy brown braid. "Hazel is older than you. Old enough to understand."

Sorrel opened her mouth again, but Master Bao held up a hand.

"Your argument is keeping your fellow novices from learning. If you do not have the discipline to allow them their learning, then you do not have the discipline to learn yourself.

Sorrel's mouth snapped closed.

"Go. Back to your lessons, little one."

Sorrel breathed in through her nose and out through her mouth. Strength in, loyalty out.

She did have the discipline to learn. She'd already learned so much. It wasn't her fault she was so short that was all people noticed.

But arguing with Master Bao had never gotten her anywhere. This was just the latest in a long line of head-butting. And she might have been young but she was smart enough to know when she was beaten.

She shuffled back to the wall.

Hazel caught her eye and gave her a sympathetic shrug, but it didn't help.

She dragged her feet toward the library where Father Naemon still lectured. Her mind raced but not along the path her teachers wanted it to take.

Master Bao didn't think she was disciplined. Well, Father Naemon talked about discipline a lot. It was kind of like loyalty. Loyalty to an idea rather than a person. That was easy enough for

Sorrel to understand. As long as the idea was fighting and not sitting at a desk during her lessons.

But if arguments didn't work on Master Bao...then she'd just have to show him.

She passed into the refectory, but instead of climbing the stairs to the library, Sorrel trotted straight through to the other side of the building and out the door.

The path sloped down from the threshold, and Sorrel could see all the way down to the valley floor below. The village lay nestled down there, past the terraced fields that lay between it and the monastery on the peak.

Heights were all Sorrel had known. Since her unknown parents had dropped her off on the monastery doorstep as a baby, she'd grown up in the mountains, looking down at the tiny people working the fields below. It made her feel tall, like her height didn't matter.

Sorrel turned at the door and stared up at the wall of the refectory. Bits of mortar flaked between the massive stones, giving it a patchy sort of feel. The monastery might have been well built but centuries and weather made their mark, and Brother Mortimer hadn't made it to this side with his repair men, yet.

Sorrel kicked off the over large sandals and set her fingers into the gaping cracks between stone blocks. Crumbling mortar scattered the grass at her feet, but she set her teeth and began to climb.

Just like a ladder. She didn't even have to stretch for her next handhold. She climbed past the refectory windows where the scent of baked ham wafted from the tables. When she reached the upper story, she paused to catch her breath just outside the library. Father Naemon droned away, oblivious to the tiny figure hanging on the windowsill.

Sorrel moved on. The tiles at the edges of the roof stuck out a bit, and she had to leap backward to catch them. Her feet swung, and she glanced down to see the valley swaying between her toes.

Sorrel grinned and pulled herself up.

Easy as cake.

She trotted to the edge of the roof where she could see Master Bao clearly. No gray-clad monks to peer through here. She had the best view and his voice carried right up the wall to her.

She centered herself like he'd said, breathing in and out and planting her bare feet on the tile roof.

Then she copied his movements, bringing her left leg up and unfurling it, slow and controlled to the side.

"Let your voice carry the power of your blow," Master Bao said. "Ha." The staccato sound emphasized his strike.

Sorrel struck out and tried to make her voice carry, too.

A couple monks looked up from the courtyard.

Sorrel kept her focus on Master Bao.

One of the monks pointed. It might have been Hazel but it was hard to tell from up here.

Master Bao stopped and turned to see what was causing the disturbance.

Sorrel kept going, practicing the kick over and over again. If the others weren't disciplined enough to ignore a distraction, that was their problem.

Laughter and gasps gathered like water in the space of the courtyard, growing to a rolling din.

She waited for Master Bao to say something, but he just stood there, hands on his hips as he stared up at her.

Father Naemon's voice carried from the library window just below the roof edge. "What's going on?"

One of the monks in the courtyard answered him, but their voice wasn't strong enough to reach Sorrel.

"Sorrel?" Father Naemon called. "Are you up there?"

"I am." It wasn't like she was trying to hide it.

"Come down from there right now. You'll hurt yourself."

She shook her head, fully aware that he couldn't see the gesture.

Father Naemon spoke to someone indoors, then raised his voice again. "I'm sending someone up to get you."

Sorrel's lips thinned as hands appeared over the edge of the roof. Brother Ferell's round face rose over his white knuckles.

Down below, Master Bao slid into another position. He kept his eyes on her as he slid his left foot back and right foot forward, his hands held palm to palm in front of his chest.

Sorrel mimicked his pose.

Master Bao curled his fists and punched out.

Sorrel punched.

Brother Ferell huffed and puffed and heaved himself over the edge of the roof, rolling up the shallow slope. He hauled himself to his feet.

Sorrel dropped Master Bao's pose and darted away across the roofs before Brother Ferell could grab her.

He came to a stop at the edge of the refectory and braced his hands on his knees as Sorrel centered herself on the chapel roof. She took up Master Bao's pose again.

She couldn't see his expression from up here, but he did cock his head. And he slid into another form.

Sorrel copied the movement.

Brother Ferell trotted foward and made a half-hearted swipe for her.

Sorrel skipped away with a grin. She might be showing Master Bao she was disciplined, but that didn't mean she couldn't have fun doing it.

As she skidded to a stop she slid into Master Bao's last form and held his gaze.

Brother Ferell puffed to a stop a roof away, admitting defeat.

Master Bar shaded his eyes. "You've proved your point, Sorrel. Come down, now."

"You mean I win?" Sorrel called.

Master Bar shook his head. "There is no winning when there is no enemy, Sorrel."

"But you'll teach me."

His grin was wide enough that she could see it even from the rooftop. "Yes, little one. I will teach you."

Sorrel chucked the last bundle of wheat into the cart at the top of the hill and raised her hand to shield her eyes from the hot autumn sunlight. She breathed in deep and stretched. She might have had her full growth now, but her head still barely reached the top of the cart.

"Idle hands make stray thoughts," Father Naemon said as he passed the highest terrace where Sorrel, Tallah, and Hazel worked.

"Yes, Father Naemon." Sorrel rolled her eyes, confident the ancient abbot couldn't see far enough to notice. He didn't even look up from his feet as he shuffled down the path that led from the monastery to the village in the valley many terraces below.

Sorrel's eyes narrowed. The abbot had been a million years old for as long as she could remember, but the last few months had changed him more than even the last decade. His once thick white hair had grown thin and wiry, and the skin that stretched across his knobbly knuckles was nearly translucent.

Hazel pushed her thick brown braid over her shoulder. Even after working all morning in the sun, her curls stayed contained and away from the sweat on her forehead. "Would you like some help down to the village?" The stout dwarf stepped as if to offer her hand to the abbot.

Father Naemon glared at her, feet still moving. He raised his hand, and his gnarled fingers moved in a complicated gesture. His bent figure disappeared with a pop and reappeared halfway down the path.

"I think that's a no," Sorrel said with a grin at Hazel.

Tallah snorted and tossed another bushel of wheat into the cart. "More like, leave a crotchety old man alone." She groaned and cracked her back. "Why are we doing this menial work anyway? Don't the villagers usually tithe to us? I feel like it defeats the purpose if we do all the work."

Sorrel frowned, but Hazel answered the other novice first. "It's a way to give back to the community that supports us," she said quietly. "We can't sit up on the mountain and claim that meditation makes us worthy of having the village wait on us hand and foot."

"Meditation's over-rated anyway," Sorrel said, grabbing Hazel's bushel and tossing it in the cart for her. "Besides, this isn't so bad."

"That's because you're closer to the ground," Tallah said, her acid look pinching the pale skin between her eyebrows. Her dark hair was cut too short to hang in her face but she still swiped her forehead as if to brush it out of the way. "You don't have as far to reach."

"Hey, no short jokes," Sorrel cried. She stepped up onto the back of the cart and used its height to gaze down across the terraces to the village below. It would be a long walk past their fellow monks who toiled in the fields.

A slow grin spread across her face, her anger with Tallah immediately forgotten. "I have an idea."

"Uh oh," Hazel said, but she said it with a warm smile.

Tallah sighed heavily. "Every time you say those words something or someone gets broken. Usually you."

"I haven't broken a bone since I was fifteen," Sorrel said,

balancing on the back of the cart and planting her hands on her hips. "And even then it was only a toe. I'm loads more mature now."

"Are you?" Tallah said. "Then what's your idea?"

Sorrel patted the raised side of the cart. "We ride this baby all the way to the bottom."

Hazel laughed out loud while Tallah buried her head in her hands.

"Maxim help us," Hazel said. "You would do it, wouldn't you?"

"Think about it," Sorrel said. "It saves all that time walking. We'll be down and unloaded three times as fast, which just means we can do more work. Father Naemon is bound to approve."

"I don't know, Sorrel..." Hazel said.

"It'll be faster. And more importantly, fun." Sorrel cocked her head at the dwarf. "Come on." She held her breath. Hazel was the calm, thoughtful, and above all, responsible one. But Sorrel could almost always get her to agree as long as she used the right arguments.

Hazel bit her lip but it was to hide a smile. "Your ideas always get me into trouble," she said, climbing into the back of the cart with Sorrel.

The halfling's heart soared. "Yeah, but it's fun trouble. Which makes it worth it."

"You're both nuts." Tallah crossed her arms.

Sorrel shrugged. "Suit yourself. You were the one who was complaining about the work. If you want to do it the hard way, go for it. Meanwhile we'll be done ahead of you..."

Tallah pushed up into the back of the cart. "Move over."

Sorrel made room. "Yes, ma'am."

"Now what—"

Sorrel kicked off with both feet. The cart was a lot heavier with the three of them in it, and Sorrel could barely reach the ground, but luckily there was such a thing as gravity. And a cart standing at the top of a hill really wanted to go down.

They creaked into motion, gaining speed on the slope.

Sorrel stuck her head up over the raised sides to feel the wind against her cheeks. "Woohoo!"

"Get down, you idiot, or the next thing you'll break is your head," Tallah snapped.

Sorrel ignored her with a grin. She wanted to see where they were going.

The path lay mostly straight between them and the valley below, and both the monks and the villages kept it smooth and clear. But that didn't mean there wasn't the occasional rut.

"Ouch, get off me."

"Sorry. I was thrown."

Hazel grabbed the edges of the cart in a white knuckled grip. "Sorrel, when we get down there...how do we stop?"

"Uhhh."

"You didn't think that far ahead?" Tallah cried.

"I don't think we're going to get that far." Sorrel pointed.

The fields around them blurred, but out ahead, they could see everything coming toward them crystal clear. Father Naemon shambled along the path, head down and deaf to the rumble racing at him from behind.

"Oh my gods, we're going to kill the abbot," Hazel moaned.

"No, we're not." Sorrel swung herself over the edge of the cart and threw her weight as far out as possible. She barely made it wobble.

"I need more weight."

"Try not being a halfling," Tallah called back.

Sorrel didn't have time for an appropriate comeback.

The gate that kept the village livestock from wandering up onto the terraces and snitching the crops rushed at them. Father Naemon had left it open.

"Thank, Maxim," Sorrel muttered. She stuck out her hand and grabbed the post as it whipped by.

It nearly cost her her arm, wrenching her shoulder hard enough to send a shooting pain up her neck, but the cart tilted up on one wheel, jumping off the path and narrowly missing Father Naemon.

The cart bounced along the rutted dirt of the last terrace, jostling Sorrel where she hung. She lost her grip and rolled free of the hurtling cart.

She fetched up against the crumbling wall of the field and raised her head in time to see the cart plunge over the edge of the terrace into the village below.

A crash echoed up the mountain, and Sorrel winced.

Tallah's head popped up over the edge of the terrace and whipped around, looking for an escape. She spun and disappeared into the village.

Sorrel groaned and rolled so at least the world was right side up again. Then she dragged herself to the edge of the terrace and peered down into the village.

The cart lay in pieces, but at least the bushels of wheat seemed intact. Hazel crawled from the wreckage and sat gazing around her with dazed eyes.

"Hazel!" Father Naemon's voice didn't sound nearly so ancient now, and he moved with the speed of an angry turtle.

Tallah had already escaped. And Hazel sat alone in the middle of Sorrel's mess.

Sorrel heaved herself over the edge of the terrace and landed below with a stumble. She straightened with a grimace and trotted toward the altercation.

"Father Naemon," she called. "It wasn't her fault. It was mine."

Father Naemon stopped with his hands on his hips and raised

his gaze to the sky. But the voice that spoke next didn't belong to the abbot.

"Why doesn't that surprise me?"

Sorrel flinched.

Master Bao. The martial arts master stood in the center of the village with a crowd of other monks and the village elders. Master Bao tilted his dark head and raised his eyebrows.

Father Naemon rubbed his spotted forehead with a gnarled hand. "Sorrel, you are a full monk now. How is it I'm still pulling you out of scrapes more appropriate for a novice."

Sorrel surveyed the wreckage. "You know, it seemed like such a good idea at the time."

There was a snort. Sorrel suspected Master Bao, but he had his lips pressed thin to hide any sort of smile.

"I'm sure," Father Naemon said dryly. "But you nearly got your fellow brothers and sisters killed."

"It wasn't that bad," Hazel said faintly, still sitting with the broken pieces of cart. "Everyone is all right." She glanced around, maybe to find Tallah, and frowned to herself.

"And I didn't destroy the harvest." Sorrel gestured at the bushels that were only a little dirty. "And we did get them down here in record time. And it was fun."

"Your priorities might be a little skewed," Father Naemon said. He glanced at Master Bao.

Sorrel's shoulders drooped.

"She is your pupil," Father Naemon told Master Bao. "What punishment would be appropriate?"

Sorrel perked up. Master Bao's punishments were always disguised as exercises. Which weren't nearly so bad as helping Brother Gregor in the kitchens or cleaning out the privies.

"Early training with me," Master Bao said. "Every morning before dawn for a month."

Sorrel groaned but it was mostly for the show of it. She liked to sleep in just like any other person, but if she had to be up before the sun, training with Master Bao was about the best thing she could imagine.

Master Bao's smirk finally crept through his censure as if he knew what she was thinking.

"Maxim make it so," Father Naemon said, bowing his head over the decision.

"Make it so," the other monks murmured.

"I'll, uh, I'll clean everything up," Sorrel said. "And make sure the harvest gets where it's supposed to go."

"I can help," Hazel said, climbing to her feet and brushing debris from her tunic. "I participated in the destruction, too." She smiled at Sorrel to take the sting from her words.

Sorrel grinned. She wasn't about to take Hazel for granted, but the dwarf always helped her clean up. Even when Sorrel got her into the worst messes.

Father Naemon didn't respond or raise his head again. He looked like he was stuck praying.

Master Bao's eyes narrowed. "Father Naemon?"

Father Naemon swayed on his feet. Then his ancient knees buckled.

Sorrel lunged forward to catch him, but even bent with age, the abbot was over twice her height. She crumpled beneath him, just keeping his head from hitting the ground.

The monks around them erupted in a chorus of concern.

"Father Naemon!"

"Is he hurt?"

"What's wrong?"

Master Bao untangled the abbot's long limbs from Sorrel and rolled him to the side.

Sorrel scrambled out of the way, her throat tight. Father Naemon's face had gone pale, and in the sunlight his veins stood out stark blue. His breath whistled shallowly in and out of his lungs.

"Father Naemon?" Master Bao said.

The abbot didn't respond.

"Way to go, Sorrel," Tallah said as they stood in the refectory, waiting for an update on Father Naemon's condition. "You killed the abbot."

Sorrel's mouth dropped open. "I did not!"

"Tallah," Hazel cried. "That's not fair. Sorrel had nothing to do with Father Naemon's collapse. He's been declining for months now."

Tallah rolled her eyes. "Yeah, she just pushed him over the edge. We all know what a screw up she is."

Hazel opened her mouth to argue, but hesitated and that brief pause made Sorrel's heart drop. She searched the dwarf's face for any sign of reassurance.

Compassion shone from Hazel's eyes but uncertainty crowded in as well.

Sorrel glanced around the refectory.

Most of the monks gathered there, waiting for news about the abbot. The ones who didn't have jobs elsewhere sat on the benches or perched on the edge of the tables. Those nearest them glanced at Sorrel and then away, their mouths tight.

Sorrel swallowed, wondering which of her exploits they were remembering exactly. There were so many vivid incidents to choose from.

Like the time she'd tried to help Brother Gregor gather honey and knocked over three hives, releasing all the bees. They'd gone right for the open windows of the library.

Or there was the time she'd convinced Brother Ferell to let

the novices study outdoors and the entire collection of Jodin Battlecalled's chronicles had blown across the fields. They'd spent hours collecting the loose pages from among the grain.

But it wasn't like those were bad ideas. Just great ideas that had gone really, really wrong.

Still, their eyes bored into the back of Sorrel's neck, making it tingle.

A collective murmur went through the monks, and Hazel and Tallah turned toward the stairs. Sorrel hopped up on a bench to see.

Master Bao helped Father Naemon shuffle down the steps and into the refectory.

Sorrel held her breath.

The abbot's color hadn't improved since he'd collapsed in the village, but on the bright side, he was upright and moving. So she couldn't have come that close to killing him. Could she?

The martial arts master helped Father Naemon to the lectern at the front of the room, leaving the abbot to clutch the edges with trembling, white hands. Master Bao retreated to the side of the room but remained alert as if ready in case the abbot decided to keel over again.

Father Naemon surveyed the monks assembled, his eyes steady but filled with emotion. They settled on Sorrel for a moment, and his lips twitched in a subdued smile.

"My friends," he said, voice quiet, but not a single monk would have dared make any noise loud enough to drown him out. "It's time for a new abbot."

The monks shifted and murmured. Sorrel exchanged a look with Hazel. The news was abrupt but not exactly surprising.

"It's time," Father Naemon said and everyone stilled again. "Time for me to commune with Maxim."

The rest settled, nodding in agreement but Sorrel bit her lip. Monks didn't just work until they dropped dead. And they didn't lay down and wait for it peacefully in their beds either. They went into the abandoned places of the world to meditate, to be closer to their god. Until their god claimed them.

At least that's what the monks called it. Anyone else would have called it dying of starvation and exposure.

It had never sat right with Sorrel, just giving up like that. But none of the other monks voiced a protest. And Father Naemon was so old. Maybe, if she tried really hard, she could imagine being that tired. That done with the world.

Father Naemon held up his hand. "Yes, it's time for a new abbot. But…I will not be doing this the normal way. Maxim has granted me some foresight. I see upheaval coming to the world. A time of trial and challenge. The monastery will need strong leadership to survive. Someone who represents strength and loyalty in the way that Maxim has taught us. So I'm setting a task. Long ago, the founder of our order, Jodin Battlecalled, stored a great artifact under our monastery. The head of Maxim's Warhammer. He placed many trials around the mighty weapon designed to find one worthy of wielding it."

Father Naemon paused, his sense of drama unaffected by his recent illness.

"Whoever goes into the catacombs and returns with the weapon will be the new abbot or abbess."

Sorrel's chest swelled as the monks around them took a collective breath. She'd never envisioned herself as an abbess before. And to be honest, she still didn't. But the call of adventure was undeniable. Strength and loyalty. Who wouldn't be drawn to a quest to prove their strength and loyalty?

And she might not be a good abbess, but she knew someone who would. Her eyes slid to Hazel.

"This is my last stricture as abbot," Father Naemon said. "Everyone here, down to the last monk must swear to abide by this decision. They must swear to follow this new leader of the monastery. Into peace or into battle, whatever Maxim brings us. Do I have your oaths?"

"We so swear." Sorrel said the words with everyone else, a shiver going through her as they left her lips. Maxim was the Greater Virtue of Loyalty as well as Strength. He hated oath-breakers especially because nothing was worse than breaking loyalty.

Father Naemon swayed on his feet, and Master Bao sprang forward to support the ancient abbot.

Father Naemon managed to raise his chin one last time. "Go, my friends. Decide who to send. I place you in Maxim's hands."

FOUR

THE MONKS SPENT the rest of the evening debating who to send into the catacombs, eventually deciding on Brother Ferell, the bookish librarian who often served at Father Naemon's side. The older monks did not ask the opinion of the younger ones.

As Brother Ferell retreated to the dormitories to rest before his trials, Tallah crossed her arms and humphed.

"They aren't even going to give us a chance," she said.

Hazel spoke in calming tones. "Well, we were novices not that long ago."

Tallah waved a hand. "That shouldn't have anything to do with it. It's a trial, isn't it? With divine components. Maxim gets to decide who the next abbot or abbess is. But they just picked one candidate to send in, ensuring that their choice comes out victorious."

"If he comes out at all," Hazel said quietly. "He'll have no help in there."

Sorrel was convinced Hazel would end up with a permanent worry line down the center of her forehead before she was twenty-two. She carried the weight of the monastery on her young shoulders.

"It should be Maxim's decision. Not theirs." Tallah pouted.

Sorrel sighed. Tallah just said that because she wanted a chance to be abbess. For once, Sorrel herself didn't have much to say.

Night clouded the clerestory windows above them as the older monks filed out of the refectory, heading for their beds. Sorrel caught a glimpse of Master Bao against the wall behind the lectern. He'd helped Father Naemon back to his rooms but he'd reappeared about halfway through the debate over who would go into the catacombs. The martial arts master had remained quiet against the wall, not interfering.

Sorrel hopped off the table and trotted over to him.

"How's Father Naemon?" she asked quietly.

Master Bao's lips pulled thin. "Not well. I don't believe he will last the night. He's gone to the mountainside to meditate."

Sorrel's mouth dropped open. "Already? Won't he wait to see if Brother Ferell is successful?"

"He doesn't have that much time, little one. I've told him and told him not to push himself these last few years. But he was always more stubborn than me, even if he was more quiet about it."

Sorrel dug the toe of her sandal into the flagstones. "Did I really kill him?"

Master Bao snorted. "Do you think a wayward young monk could kill someone like Father Naemon?" he said. "You are a good fighter, Sorrel, though you have your faults. You act without thinking and you throw too much of yourself into things. But you are nothing Father Naemon could not handle."

Sorrel's shoulders sagged, releasing a tension she hadn't realized she'd been carrying. "I wish I'd listened to him more, now. I didn't even get to say goodbye."

"No one did. He slipped out while the rest were debating who to send. He wanted it that way. He always led without a fuss, he would not have wanted a fuss made over his departure, either."

Sorrel's eyes narrowed on her toes. "Why didn't they pick you to go to the catacombs?"

Master Bao's lips twisted. "I told them not to."

Her mouth dropped open. "Why?"

He laughed, throwing his head back so his white beard shook. "You think I would make a good abbot?"

"I think you're the one with the best chance of returning with the Warhammer. And that's what Father Naemon said counted, so..."

He looked down at her, mirth fading, replaced with a more contemplative look.

"I am not a leader, Sorrel. I am a teacher. I am servant. A bulwark for those who are wiser than me. When Father Naemon needed something done, I was the one to make it happen."

Sorrel screwed up her nose. "That's not very heroic," she said, thinking of all the legends surrounding Jodin Battlecalled.

"Perhaps it's the most heroic," Master Bao said. "Doing something because it has to be done, because you are good at it with no hope of glory or accolades. Simply supporting another person. There is great honor in being who you are supposed to be."

"And you're a bulwark," she said. She glanced at the empty doorframe where the night air drifted into the refectory. "You think that Brother Ferell is the one you're supposed to be supporting?"

Master Bao's gaze followed hers. "I will abide by Father Naemon's decision and Maxim's proclamation. Whoever comes out of the catacombs with the Warhammer is my new abbot. That is what I swore. As did you."

He turned to retreat back up the steps to the library.

Sorrel rolled her eyes. "I'm not trying to get out of it," she called after him.

He didn't pause, but he did throw a grin over his shoulder at her.

Sorrel turned back to Tallah and Hazel, chewing her lip while she thought about honor and bulwarks and propping up someone else who might be better at something than you were.

She would make a terrible abbess. Everything Master Bao said was true, and she accepted that with a shrug. She was impulsive and tended to jump into things with both feet, leaving nowhere to stand firm. But she knew that she was strong. She was strong enough to support the one she chose. And Brother Ferell wasn't it.

Sure, he was wise and kind and made a great librarian. And he looked like a stork when he chased papers across the fields. But he wasn't the one who would have the calm and the compassion to lead the monastery through whatever hardships Father Naemon had seen. He tended to panic over little things, like paper chasing.

But Hazel had always been the voice of calm and reason. She was compassion where Sorrel was impatience. She was gentle where Sorrel was fierce.

"And who says we're not wise," Tallah said. Still whining. "Who says we're not strong and loyal just like the rest of them. Just because we're young. We should have the same chance as the others."

"Are you saying everyone should go down there and risk themselves?" Hazel said. "Even the novices?"

Tallah waved her hand. "I'm saying they should let anyone who wants to take their chance."

"Then maybe we should," Sorrel said, sliding into the conversation as smoothly as she slid under Tallah's guard in the practice ring.

Tallah and Hazel blinked at her. "What?"

"Maybe that's part of the test," Sorrel said with shrug. "We have to follow whoever comes out of there with the Warhammer. But Father Naemon never said anything about limiting who went in."

Tallah's gaze grew distant as she stared over Sorrel's shoulder, considering the words. But she wasn't the one who would balk.

Sorrel let her eyes rest on Hazel's worried face.

"If we go, too, then we can help Brother Ferell," she said. "We can be there if he gets hurt, which you know he will."

She shifted her gaze to Tallah. "And we'll have a chance at the Warhammer, too." That's all Tallah really cared about anyway. She wouldn't be the one pulling Brother Ferell out of any trouble if this morning was anything to go by.

"We can strike twice with the same weapon," she said, using one of Master Bao's favorite idioms.

And she could help Hazel get to the Warhammer. She could be the dwarf's bulwark. Just like Master Bao and Father Naemon.

At least it wasn't like they had to sneak through some grate in the floor or climb down the privy chute to get to the catacombs. There was a wide archway at the back of the chapel that led down into the underbelly of the monastery. Sconces lined the passage. None of them were lit, yet, but at least there was the promise of light.

The monks of Maxim's monastery gathered in the chapel to give their blessings to Brother Ferell.

Sorrel, Hazel, and Tallah stood unnoticed in the background.

The only one who made eye contact was Master Bao, and

Sorrel just gave him a wide grin and twiddled her fingers. *Nothing to see here. Just a couple of monks doing their duty.*

It took forever for the rest of them to send Brother Ferell off. But eventually the librarian started down the steps. The sconces lit by themselves as he passed.

"Neat," Sorrel said under her breath. That little bit of ancient magic could help them so long as it worked for everyone.

Hazel's idea had been to wait to follow Brother Ferell until all the monks had gone back to their duties, but neither Sorrel nor Tallah believed that would happen. Some might go away—Brother Gregor had lunch to prepare after all—but they guessed that the rest would stick around until Brother Ferell either returned or...didn't.

And they couldn't wait that long.

"What now?" Tallah whispered. "We can't just sit here forever, Sorrel."

"Just give it two seconds. You know patience is one of the Greater Virtues."

Hazel glanced up to the frieze that decorated the top of the wall, her eyes seeking out Illias, goddess of Patience, but Tallah's lips twisted in a sneer.

"If this doesn't work, I'm taking ove—"

Before she could finish, a candle across the chapel spluttered. The same candle Sorrel had surreptitiously replaced as all the other monks had been distracted.

She grinned in anticipation.

The candle fizzled. Then exploded in a shower of sparks.

The gathered monks cried out and turned to face the threat, just as Sorrel, Hazel, and Tallah slipped along the far wall and down the steps after Brother Ferell.

"Ha!" Sorrel said as they raced down below. "I kind of wish we could stay to see the aftermath."

"No one will be hurt, will they?" Hazel cast a glance over her shoulder.

"Pssh, it was just a sparkler from the workshop. That one spurt is all it has in it. We only needed two seconds, not two minutes."

"Yeah, yeah, great idea," Tallah said. "My plan would have worked, too, you know."

"Maybe, but we would never have been able to get the stink out," Sorrel said. "Those pest grenades are potent."

"Sorrel!" Brother Gregor's distant cry carried down the stone tunnel, his outrage nipping at their heels.

Sorrel paused on a step. "How'd he know it was me?"

Tallah pinched her elbow to keep her moving. "Because it's always you."

"It's *usually* me. There's a difference between usually and always."

They reached the bottom of the stairs and peered into the space beneath the chapel. Tombs lined the walls, decorated with effigies of past abbots.

The actual bodies weren't there, since the abbots went out to meditate themselves to death. But Sorrel still shivered with the feeling that they weren't entirely alone.

At the very back of the room stood a statue of Jodin Battle-called, a paladin of Maxim and the founder of their order. He faced the wall, his entire statue cocked on its plinth to reveal a passage behind him, leading down into the catacombs proper.

Sorrel smiled and skipped to the statue. "It's just like a quest," she said to herself and slapped Jodin's knee for luck.

Then she jerked her head at the other two. The sconces in this tunnel were already lit as well. Brother Ferell was making good time on his long spindly legs.

The way sloped downward, this time without stairs. Just the

closely fitted flagstones that grew slick with moisture as they passed deeper into the earth.

The tunnel finally leveled out and the ceiling soared above into a massive cavern, but the way ahead was blocked. Their passage split into three choices instead of opening up the way the ceiling seemed to indicate.

The sconces down the left path were lit.

"It's a maze," Hazel said. "The first trial is a maze."

Sorrel tapped her teeth, thinking back to all those summer afternoons in the library with Father Naemon.

"Strength and loyalty," she said. "Jodin Battlecalled would have set up trials to test our strength and loyalty according to Maxim's precepts. And strength comes in three varieties."

"Strength of mind, strength of body, strength of will," Tallah said.

Sorrel cocked her head. "Good job. Didn't know if you remembered."

"I took the same classes as you," Tallah snapped. "And I didn't sneak out as often."

Sorrel rolled her eyes. "I only sneaked out when I already knew the lesson."

"Or if there was something more interesting outside," Hazel said with a playful smile.

"Well, obviously."

"So this maze is the strength of mind trial," Tallah said, then snorted. "This will be easy. We just follow Brother Ferell's path."

She headed for the lit passageway.

The sconce extinguished itself, leaving the three of them in the dark.

"Something tells me Jodin Battlecalled might have been smarter than that," Sorrel said.

"Uh, did anyone think to bring a light?" Hazel asked.

"No. That would have actually made sense," Sorrel said. "And we don't generally do the things that make sense."

"Speak for yourself," Tallah said.

"How do we get through?" Hazel ran her hand along the wall and headed for the left passage. "We know the first turn, assuming Brother Ferell was right. But he must have had something to go on. Some clue."

Tallah followed Hazel down the left branching while Sorrel stared up at the walls. They were slick with moisture and stretched three times Tallah's height. But then they stopped, and the roof disappeared in the darkness far above that.

"We could copy Brother Ferell," Sorrel said. "Or we could do this our own way."

Hazel's head popped around the corner again. "What's our own way?"

"Look at the problem from above." Sorrel grinned and then ran at the wall.

"You're never getting up that," Tallah said. "It's too slippery."

Sorrel hit the wall running, and launched herself upward several feet. Her hands caught at the cracks between blocks of stone, and she clung there, triumph coursing through her veins.

"Watch me," she said.

She heaved herself higher and the cracks and handholds seemed to open up before her, almost like Jodin Battlecalled had provided a way forward for someone clever enough to think outside the closed in passages of the maze.

Sorrel scampered the last few feet and hauled herself to the top of the wall. With her eyes getting used to the dark, she saw the cavern opening around them. Walls snaked away from the tunnel that led back up to the monastery, their crazy design cutting the cavern into dozens of narrow passageways.

Below, Hazel ran her hand over the wall, frown lines marring her forehead. "I don't think we'll be able to get up there."

Tallah opened her mouth as if to protest and then eyed the wall with a scowl. "Probably not. Everyone knows Sorrel's the best at escaping her problems by climbing over them."

"You say that like it's an insult," Sorrel said, gazing down at them with her feet swinging. "But I'm the one up here while you're stuck down there."

Tallah's face flushed in the dark as Sorrel climbed to her feet.

"You don't have to climb up," Sorrel said. "I'll lead you through. I can see the dead ends from here."

And off in the distance a light bobbed, bouncing from the angled walls. Brother Ferell. He was nearing the end of the maze where the walls opened onto an area Sorrel couldn't see.

"He was smart enough to bring his own light," she muttered then she raised her voice. "This way."

Hazel and Tallah trailed along with her as Sorrel made her way along the top of the wall. She took one wrong turn and had to leap across the passageway to another wall three times, but eventually they made it to the end. The tunnel where Hazel and Tallah walked opened onto a wide chasm spanned by a narrow rock bridge. Brother Ferell's light bobbed somewhere on the other side.

Hazel and Tallah paused at the edge of the chasm as Sorrel hopped down from the top of the wall.

"Ha," she said. "Easy as cake."

"You've never made cake in your life," Tallah said.

Sorrel tilted her head. "I helped Brother Gregor once."

"What do you suppose is next?" Hazel asked. "Strength of body?"

"How do you test strength of body?" Tallah said.

Sorrel shrugged. "Master Bao always has us do exercises. But whatever it is, I'll bet it's on the other side."

Without hesitation, she headed across the bridge.

"Oooh," Hazel said, following. "I don't like this."

"Yeah, don't look down." Sorrel didn't bother following her own advice and leaned over to peer into the chasm. There was no discernible bottom.

"Would you stop that?" Hazel cried. "What if you slip?"

"I won't slip. I've been climbing around on rooftops and mountains since I was four."

"It's a lot different to fall from a roof or a mountain than into a bottomless pit."

"Why?" Sorrel asked. "You're dead either way. What does it matter how far you fall first?"

"Can we not talk about falling while walking over said bottomless pit?" Tallah growled from the rear.

Sorrel opened her mouth to tease them some more, but a scream split the air, echoing from the cavern's distant walls.

"Brother Ferell," Hazel said with a gasp.

Sorrel was already running. She sprinted the last few feet across the bridge and into the open space beyond. Here the cavern opened onto a vast plateau nearly as big as the village below the monastery.

A light flickered against the far wall and shadows danced on the stone, too big and amorphous to make out.

As she raced forward, Sorrel squinted. A torch lay on the ground, illuminating a large shadow which thrashed. The big shadow threw a gray-clad figure against the wall.

Brother Ferell slid down with a groan.

Sorrel pulled her quarterstaff from her back. "Hazel, get to Brother Ferell," she called. "Tallah, with me."

Ten feet away she took a flying leap at the shadow, staff over her head.

She screamed as she struck.

Her staff connected with a solid thwack and the shadow shrieked. It spun to face Sorrel, and the light from the torch bounced off shining scales, giving her a glimpse of a sharp snout and long fangs. The creature towered over her, raising huge membranous wings.

"Is…that a winged viper?" Tallah said, skidding up beside her.

"That's what I'm seeing. It probably has some cool name but—"

The viper struck, and Sorrel threw herself to one side while Tallah rolled away on the other.

Hazel didn't slow down. She just swerved around the vicious fangs and made straight for Brother Ferell, who lay unmoving against the stone.

"Okay. I'll take left, you take right," Sorrel called to Tallah as soon as she'd sprung to her feet. She raced for the creature's left side.

The tail whipped around, but Sorrel dove over it and came up on the other side running.

Tallah cried out as the scaly coils bunched and the creature lunged for her. Sorrel took the opportunity and leaped to the viper's back. She scrambled up the slippery scales and aimed a blow at the left wing, right where the joint met its spine.

The viper shrieked and twisted all the way around until suddenly Sorrel was dodging teeth from its back. She staggered back, sliding down the spine.

"Flexible bugger, aren't you?"

She planted her feet and swung her staff like a club, knocking a fang clean off.

The viper hissed and snapped its jaw shut. The remaining teeth just missed Sorrel, but they snagged in her tunic, and the creature dragged her from its back.

Sorrel dangled in the air, thirty feet over the ground. Beneath her, Tallah scrambled to strike at the viper's body.

The viper shook its head, and Sorrel swung wildly. Her tunic tore with a resounding rip, and the cavern spun, making her stomach lurch.

Sorrel moaned. "Oh, I'm going to barf."

She flailed wildly, and her hand caught hold of something hot and scaly. Without stopping to think any further, she scrambled up, using her new handhold. She tore her tunic free from its teeth, and when she blinked she found herself straddling the viper's snout, her hand in its nostril and her feet braced on its lips.

"Well, since I'm here," she said and brought her staff down between its eyes.

The viper jerked, but Sorrel was already scrambling higher, and with a flourish, she bashed it on the head one more time.

The viper collapsed, and Sorrel fell with it.

She rolled across the stone floor below and came up panting, her staff ready.

But the viper lay still.

Tallah stared at the long snaking body, her weapon ready in her hand as well. Then she looked at Sorrel.

"Is it dead?"

"As dead as I can make it," Sorrel said. "Unless you want to bash it one more time for good measure."

"Do you think it's been here since Jodin Battlecalled set up the trials?"

Sorrel nudged the creature with her staff. "I guess anything's possible with enough magic."

"Sorrel, Tallah. You'd better come here," Hazel called and something in her voice made Sorrel drop her staff and run.

Hazel knelt at the back wall, Brother Ferell's head in her lap. The librarian blinked at the ceiling blearily. A trickle of red crept down his temple and the side of his face.

"Is he going to be okay?" Sorrel asked.

"I don't know," Hazel said. "He's opened his eyes, so that's a good sign. But we need to get him to the infirmary."

"No way," Tallah said. "I'm not leaving the trials now. We're so close."

Hazel's eyes flashed. "I'm not asking you to. I'll go with him. If you feel like this test is more important than a life, then by all means, keep going."

Tallah flushed.

Hazel glanced at Sorrel.

Sorrel bit her lip, her breath coming faster. If Hazel left with Brother Ferell, how would she retrieve the Warhammer? How would Sorrel help her become the next abbess?

But Hazel was right. They couldn't leave Brother Ferell here. And they definitely couldn't bring him along with them. He needed help. If only they could convince Tallah to take him, but that would be like squeezing lemon juice from a rock.

Sorrel squared her shoulders. She'd just have to get the Warhammer for Hazel herself. And then give it to her. Maxim could hardly object to that. That's what loyalty was, wasn't it?

And as long as Hazel was the one to present it to the monks, it would fulfill Father Naemon's last request. Hazel would be named the new abbess, and the monastery would be prepared to face whatever hardship was ahead.

"I'll help you get him across the bridge," Sorrel said quietly as Tallah turned on her heel with a huff.

Hazel's lips thinned, but she nodded.

Sorrel didn't like that little sign of disappointment, but Hazel would understand when she returned with the Warhammer.

Together they put their shoulders under Brother Ferell's arms and helped him upright. Hazel was a dwarf and Sorrel a halfling so he towered over the two of them, but they made it work, half walking, half dragging him to the bridge.

Hazel kept her gaze firmly on the ground in front of them as they crossed and Sorrel made sure to grip Brother Ferell's tunic tightly to keep him from straying too far to either side.

At the entrance of the maze, Hazel paused.

Sorrel slipped out from under Brother Ferell's arm. "I'll be back in no time with the Warhammer," she said.

"I don't care about some silly hammer," Hazel said without meeting her eyes. "I just want you both to come back safely."

Sorrel opened her mouth, not sure what she would say, but Hazel disappeared into the maze, guiding Brother Ferell's faltering steps.

Sorrel stared at the empty hallway for another second or two before turning and hurrying back across the bridge and the empty plateau with the viper corpse. Tallah had already found the next passageway, a tunnel opening in the back wall, clearly guarded by the dead viper.

Sorrel raced to catch up.

Tallah gave her a look as she came even with her. She'd scooped up Brother Ferell's abandoned torch, and its flickering light lit up the suspicious planes of her face.

"I wouldn't think you'd be interested in getting the Warhammer," she said. "You don't seem like much of a leader to me."

More of a leader than you, Sorrel thought to herself. *And Hazel's a better leader than either of us combined. That's the important thing.*

She didn't say any of that. Instead, she shrugged. "I'm in it for the adventure. Jodin Battlecalled walked these halls once. Can you imagine?"

Tallah rolled her eyes.

A gust of air struck them like a moving wall and the torch snuffed out.

Sorrel gasped, falling to her hands and knees to avoid being bowled over and down the hallway they'd come through. The wind buffeted her torn tunic, and she raised a hand to protect her eyes as she peered ahead.

The tunnel stretched on, exactly the same as it had been before, but the wind pounded through it, whipping against the walls, creating a storm strong enough to blow them backwards.

Tallah had dropped to all fours as well and clung to the floor with her eyes closed.

Far ahead, a light pulsed at the end of the tunnel.

Sorrel put her head down and started crawling. One hand in front of the other, her fingers and toes digging into the rock to keep her steady.

"What is this?" Tallah shouted, the wind tearing her words away and tossing them down the tunnel.

"Strength of will," Sorrel said. "How stubborn are you, Tallah?" She cast a fierce grin over her shoulder.

Tallah grimaced at her and started crawling.

Sorrel's arms burned, but the wind seemed designed to take her to the edge of her endurance but no further. She just had to keep going, keep crawling, until it ended.

Oh gods, what if it never ended? Or what if Maxim really didn't want her reaching the Warhammer? This wind could keep going until she gave up out of exhaustion or frustration.

Sorrel gritted her teeth. She wasn't doing this for herself. She was doing this for Hazel. She was doing it for the monks, who needed someone like the dwarf to lead them. Surely Maxim knew that.

Her eyes watered, and she squeezed them shut. If she kept her shoulder to the wall, she didn't need to see where she was going anyway. The tunnel was straight enough. She just had to make it to the end.

A particularly fierce gust made her slip, and she dug in her fingers and toes.

Not giving up, she told the wind.

She bared her teeth and heaved herself forward…

And popped into a pocket of calm.

She rolled onto her back, gasping. Her fingers stung, and she had to blink water out of her eyes, but the wind didn't try to blow her away anymore.

A square room surrounded her lit by candles that remained perfectly still in the quiet air. More magic.

She turned her head to check Tallah.

The other monk was still stuck in the tunnel, arms straining, just feet away from the threshold where she'd find rest. But she held there, too tired to move forward and too stubborn to let go.

Sorrel's lips pressed together. She could go on alone. This would be her chance to rid herself of Tallah.

But the thought made her gut squirm. She could just imagine the disappointment on Hazel's face.

And it wasn't like Tallah was actually evil. She was just…not very nice.

Sorrel sighed and held out her bloody hand. "Tallah," she called. "Come on. You can do it."

Tallah's eyes cracked open and fastened on Sorrel's fingers, which waggled just a few inches from her nose.

"You can do it," Sorrel said again.

Tallah strained and got one arm forward enough to grip Sorrel's hand.

Sorrel heaved and yanked the other monk into the square room. The roar from the wind died abruptly, leaving Sorrel's ears ringing.

Tallah lay on the floor, her chest heaving. Sorrel gave her a minute.

"Thank you," Tallah finally said, sounding small and faint.

"You're welcome." And Sorrel very heroically didn't rub it in.

She propped herself up on her elbows and examined the room more closely. A wire fence divided the whole thing in half, and on the other side, she could just make out a pedestal.

She climbed to her feet, Tallah a second behind her.

On the pedestal behind the fence rested a rectangular metal shape. Square on one end and wickedly pointed on the other, decorated with a stylized sunburst and knots to represent the ties that bound the monks together.

"Maxim's Warhammer," Tallah breathed.

"Well, just the head," Sorrel said, planting her hands on her hips.

"Yes, I know just the head," Tallah snapped. "But that's the important part right now."

The head rested on the pedestal as if waiting for the shaft that would make it whole again. There was even a notch in the top where the two pieces would join.

Sorrel stepped closer to the fence, examining the barrier. The wire was spaced wide enough to see through, but even Sorrel wasn't small enough to squeeze between the gaps, and the fence itself stretched from one side of the room to the other with no way around.

The stone floor was unrelieved marble, except for one square of blue directly opposite the pedestal.

Could be a trap, but that so far that hadn't really been Jodin Battlecalled's style. And nothing would happen if they stood here gawking for all eternity.

Sorrel stepped on the square.

A click above their heads made her look up.

A pocket appeared in the wire fence all the way at the top. Just big enough for someone to climb through.

She grinned.

But the moment she stepped off the square, the gap closed again, leaving unrelieved wire fencing.

"A puzzle?" Tallah said, staring up where the gap had been.

Sorrel glanced between the Warhammer, the square, and Tallah. Then she sighed. "Another test," she said. "One of us has to stay here while the other goes over to retrieve the Warhammer."

Tallah's gaze locked avidly on the metal head, but then she glanced up at the fence and her face fell.

"I can't make that climb," she said with as much humility as Sorrel had ever heard from her. "Not after the hallway."

Sorrel softened just a little. She glanced down at her bloody palms. They stung, but they'd carry her a little further today.

"I can make it if you'll hold the way open for me."

Tallah gave her a short sharp nod.

Sorrel set her damaged hands on the fence and began to climb. She didn't have the energy to scramble up like normal, but she made it to the top just as Tallah stepped on the square. The gap clicked open, and she shimmied through. On the other side, she climbed down just far enough she could drop the rest of the way and rubbed her palms on her pants, leaving streaks of blood.

Then she took a deep breath and faced the pedestal. This was it. The Warhammer was right there, reflecting the candlelight, and all she had to do was take it.

She placed her hands on the cool metal. "Thanks, Maxim," she said under her breath. And she lifted it free.

Above her, the gap in the fence clicked shut.

Sorrel frowned up at it. "That's…not what I was expecting."

She'd expected it to stay open, forcing her to trust Tallah long enough for her to carry the Warhammer back over.

Directly in front of her nose, another gap appeared. Just large enough to pass the head of the Warhammer through.

"Oh," she said flatly.

Tallah's eyes met hers.

Loyalty. The final aspect of the Greater Virtue they both followed.

She had to hand the head of the Warhammer over and trust that Tallah was loyal to her and to Father Naemon's decree.

Her thumb stroked over one of the knots carved into the surface of the metal, leaving a little smear of blood.

She looked down at it one last time. Sorrel wasn't really a warhammer kind of girl, but it was beautiful in its own way. And it belonged to her god. To Maxim, the Greater Virtue of Strength and Loyalty. She'd proven her strength. Now he would prove his loyalty and not let her make the wrong decision. Right?

She held the head out through the gap in the fence.

Tallah took it. And waited.

As soon as the head was through the fence, the gap above their heads clicked open once more, allowing Sorrel a way to leave.

She blew out her breath as Tallah still stood there, waiting for her. Then she huffed a laugh and started climbing. She'd been silly to doubt. Tallah was a monk first, no matter how mean. And she'd never done anything to outright hurt Sorrel.

She reached the gap and climbed through. Her arms shook with exhaustion. Maybe she'd suggest the wind trick to Master Bao if he wanted his trainees to work on strengthening their arms.

She dropped to the floor in front of the square and dusted off her hands. "Okay," she said. "Let's get out of here."

She turned.

The room was empty and Tallah was gone. With the Warhammer.

By the time Sorrel climbed back up to the monastery, her feet dragging with dread and weariness, the damage was done. She came out of the dark depths of the tunnel to find the monks gathered in the chapel, surrounding Tallah, who held the head of Maxim's Warhammer above her head.

She didn't even look winded. Had she really been that exhausted after crawling through the wind tunnel? Or had she been faking it?

"Congratulations, Abbess," Brother Gregor was saying. "Father Naemon would be proud. And I'm sure as soon as Brother Ferell recovers, he and Master Bao will have gathered everything you need for a smooth transition."

"Wait," Sorrel said from the entrance of the tunnel. She still had a hand against the wall to keep herself upright.

This wasn't how it was supposed to go. She'd gotten the Warhammer for Hazel. Not Tallah. Her throat burned as the monks turned to her with varying expressions of surprise and exasperation.

"Sorrel," Brother Gregor said on a huff of breath. "There you are. You've caused quite enough trouble already today."

And she was about to cause some more.

"This isn't right," Sorrel said, following the yank in her gut. "She shouldn't be abbess."

A gasp went through the gathered monks, and Brother Gregor's jowls pulled in a heavy frown.

"Sorrel," Master Bao said. He stood against the altar, arms crossed. "Think carefully about what you're going to say."

"You swore to Father Naemon as he stood dying to follow whoever came out of the catacombs wielding Maxim's weapon," Brother Gregor said. "Your words here could make you an oath-breaker."

"I'm standing here, holding the weapon, Sorrel," Tallah said, raising her chin. "Can you deny that?"

"No, but you didn't retrieve it. I did. I made it through the trials. I was the one who grabbed it off the pedestal." And Tallah hadn't shown any loyalty by running off with it. She'd betrayed Sorrel. Someone like that should never be an abbess.

Tallah's face fell like she was disappointed, and she shook her head. "Sorrel, I know we've had our differences. But don't ruin your life for this one lie."

Sorrel staggered backward a step, cold spreading from her stomach up through her chest.

Liar.

She'd been called many things at the monastery. Imp, troublemaker, trickster. But never liar.

"This won't change anything," Tallah said soothingly. "You'll still have your place here, and I'll treat you as well as Father Naemon ever did."

"You already haven't. I'm not the one lying. You are."

Tallah's mouth hardened. "All the proof is sitting here in my hands." She hefted the head of the Warhammer. "It's just stupid to keep denying it. I returned the weapon to the monastery. According to Father Naemon's wishes, I'm the new abbess."

Sorrel glanced desperately at Master Bao.

The old martial arts master stared hard at Tallah. "Father Naemon's wishes were clear."

"You have to admit," Tallah said to the rest of the monks, her tone conversational. "Sorrel's always stirred things up."

"A plucky troublemaker," Brother Gregor said with a rueful grin.

"That doesn't make me a liar," Sorrel cried. "Where's Hazel?" Her last hope. The one she'd pinned all her plans on.

The monks parted to reveal Hazel by the far wall. Brother Ferell lay on a thin pallet beside her. His color looked better, but there was a livid purple bruise spreading from his thinning hairline down his face.

"Hazel?" Sorrel said, voice plaintive.

Hazel didn't meet her eyes. "I wasn't there, Sorrel. I don't know what happened."

But she still could have defended Sorrel's character. She still could have said something to stop the other monks from dragging her through the mud.

Hazel wrung her hands and said without looking up, "Tallah is the one with the Warhammer. That makes it pretty clear."

"Come on," Tallah said, holding a hand out to Sorrel. "Don't make yourself an oathbreaker out of this petty grudge."

Sorrel stared at Tallah's hands, noting the blunt ends of her fingers. Her hands weren't shredded the way Sorrel's were. The head of the Warhammer glinted under her other arm, pristine and perfect and mocking her with its silence.

Tallah must have wiped the blood from it so Sorrel couldn't even use that to defend herself.

Tallah stood, hand outstretched, waiting for her to take it. Which would just be a different sort of lie. A real one, for one thing.

Be called a liar while defending the truth? Or back down and become what they already believed her to be?

Sorrel spun on her heel and stalked to the door of the chapel.

"Sorrel," Tallah called a note of command in her voice.

Sorrel ignored her and pushed through the door, breathing hard.

Outside, the moon had risen and the crisp fall air called out goosebumps along her skin. She padded to the middle of the courtyard, surrounded by the monastery walls and tilted her head up to the sky.

She wouldn't cry, though her throat ached with too many thoughts and feelings to process.

The truth…the truth was…

The truth was that she'd failed the final trial. The trial of loyalty. She couldn't count on loyalty from any of them. Not the monks, not Tallah, and not Hazel.

Tallah didn't deserve the Warhammer. But neither did Sorrel.

Her hands clenched, fingernails biting into her ragged palms. They all looked at her and saw a liar. Even though she'd never lied before. They didn't see the truth of her. They preferred to believe Tallah's warped stories.

A quiet step beside her made her flinch. The familiar scuff of a sandal didn't fill her with confidence the way it normally did.

"My hands are tied," Master Bao said into the night.

"I know."

He'd promised to uphold Father Naemon's wishes. No matter who had come out of the catacombs victorious. And if he didn't, if he risked that to defend her, then the monks would be divided for whatever hardship Father Naemon had forseen.

She didn't want him to defend her. She hadn't wanted to be abbess anyway. She'd wanted Hazel to be abbess. But maybe that hadn't been the best idea either, since she'd ended up betraying Sorrel, too. She'd been as weak against Tallah's words as the others.

Maybe Hazel really wouldn't have made a great leader. Maybe Sorrel was as blind to Hazel's faults as the monks were blind to Sorrel's strengths.

"You've never lied to me, Sorrel," Master Bao said. "But I can't prove what happened down there. You can."

Her eyes snapped open, and she tilted her head to peer at him.

"The head is only half of Maxim's Warhammer. The other half, the shaft, is somewhere in the world. Jodin Battlecalled thought it belonged out there doing good." He fixed her with his gaze. "The shaft is a powerful weapon by itself, but it becomes something special for Maxim's chosen. It will obey the owner of the head. The true owner."

Sorrel's breath hissed through her teeth.

"Strength and loyalty, Sorrel," Master Bao said and turned to walk away. That was it. That was all he said.

It was all he had to say.

"Strength and loyalty, Master Bao," she said to his back.

He disappeared back into the chapel with the others. Sorrel waited until he'd gone. Then her fingers curled into fists.

The true owner. The truth proved.

She could do that. Even alone.

She would have thought it would be harder to leave the only home she'd known. But it just left a dull ache beneath her breastbone. That would fade, right?

Because the monastery might have been her home, but the monks were no longer her family. Not if they chose to believe the worst of her.

She walked out the gate with nothing but her quarterstaff on her back.

PART THREE
LILLIE

Lillie's origin story is best read after *Trust and Treason.*

Trigger warnings for attempted rape and assault.

FIVE

Lilliara Ephyra, fourth child of Lord Ephyra, stood on her tiptoes to see the pictures. Her eldest brother, Xavier, chuckled and pulled her up onto the bed beside them. Kellan wrapped his arms around her and they leaned forward together.

Lord Ephyra smiled indulgently and tipped the book so everyone could see. Even stoic Innis snuggled in so they were all tucked together. A lesser bed would have creaked under the weight.

"And when the great knight Meridon had slain the dragon and rescued all of Southglen, he put down his sword and took his place beside the princess," Lord Ephyra intoned. The lamplight glinted from his spectacles as he squinted at the page. "In the winter he helped rule Southglen with a wise and steady hand. In the spring and summer he patrolled its borders, keeping the country safe. And in the fall he took off his armor and labored in the fields beside the harvesters."

Xavier snorted. "Why would Meridon work in the fields? With the peasants? He was a prince. The point of being a prince is that you don't have to do all that stuff."

Ephyra speared his son with a glance over the edge of his spectacles. "There are no princes in Southglen," he said. "The Thrones only choose princesses. Meridon was a consort. And the point that the author is trying to make is that power and privilege come with responsibility and a lot of hard work. Meridon had to work to keep Southglen safe. And he worked beside his people to ensure they had enough to eat for the winter."

"But why would he care?" Innis asked quietly.

"A noble's honor lies with his people," Ephyra said, mouth pulling down in a frown. "Their well being is your responsibility. If they are prosperous and healthy, then you can be proud. If they are starving, then your shame is greater than any pride you can take in your name."

Innis bit his lip and bowed his head.

Lillie touched the page where Meridon stood with his arm around a beautiful woman with long red hair. The knight wore shining armor not quite covered by a royal blue tabard.

Her father looked nothing like Meridon, but she'd always seen him as the heroic knight, anyway. Still, he was missing something. She stroked the lady's hair.

"What happened to Mama?" Lillie asked.

Ephyra hesitated long enough for Xavier to roll his eyes at his sister. "She left because she had you."

Lillie's face crumpled. She hated when Xavier's tone went all cold like that but his words made it even worse.

Kellan's arms tightened around her, but the comfort did little to take away the sting.

"Xavier," Ephyra snapped. "That is untrue and unkind and unfitting for someone of your station."

Xavier flushed, the red creeping up to his slightly pointed ears.

Lillie sniffed, holding back tears, and Ephyra took her hands. "Your mother left for her own reasons. I know you miss her." He glanced at the older boys. "But you cannot take your grief out on each other. You are family and that is stronger than any bond created by man. Remember that."

He tapped Lillie's nose to make her smile.

"Sorry, Lillie," Xavier mumbled. He reached across Kellan to give her an awkward hug.

She snuggled into his arm, breathing in the smell of leather and horse. He'd been working in the yard that afternoon, swinging his practice sword.

"And with that, I think it's time someone was in bed," Ephyra said with a broad wink.

The boys scrambled down off the fluffy mattress. Lillie reluctantly climbed up to wriggle under the covers.

Ephyra leaned over to stroke a stray lock of blonde hair from her forehead and kissed her soundly. "Goodnight, Lilliara," he said.

Then he chased the boys out and blew out the lamp.

"Not all the way closed," Lillie called as her father started to pull the door shut.

He obliged with a chuckle and left it ajar so the light from the hallway shone in. Lillie pulled her stuffed horse close and shut her eyes.

"Xavier, a word," their father said out in the hall. He always spoke like that. As if they were adults. She could imagine her eldest brother straightening. He was in that awkward stage where he was tall but his limbs didn't work quite in concert yet. He'd be a big man one day, but for now gawky was a better word.

"I said I was sorry," Xavier said, heading off the argument.

"That doesn't fix the problem." Their father spoke quietly, clearly unaware that his voice carried straight through the door into her room.

"She seemed all right."

"The problem is with you, right now." Ephyra was normally

warm and comforting when he delivered his lectures, but his voice had grown an edge Lillie didn't normally hear. Her eyes popped open in the dark.

"Xavier, you want to be a knight, and I've done my best to teach you honor and duty and chivalry, but your first duty in this home is to protect your family."

"You don't think she should learn to protect herself? Maybe it's true Mother left for her own reasons. But it was just after she was born. She'll have to learn to live with being abandoned sometime."

Ephyra sighed loud enough Lillie could hear. "Eventually, yes. But learn this now, Xavier. The world is harsh enough without us adding to it. Our job as a family is to protect one another from the world. We are a haven for each other. Because if we are not, then no place in the world is safe."

There was a silence that indicated Xavier was hanging his head.

"It's hard being the oldest," Xavier said softly.

"I know," Ephyra replied. "It seems like all the responsibilities fall on you. But I promise, one day Lilliara and the others will be old enough to protect you from the world, too. I hope I've taught you all well enough to get there someday."

Footsteps padded away down the hall, and Lillie snuggled deeper into her bed, content in the knowledge that she had her family there to keep her safe no matter what happened. Even in a harsh world, the Ephyra's stood strong, and she was a part of that.

"Your first day home from the university and of course the only thing you want to do is go to the library," Kellan said with a grin.

The front steps of the Glenhaven library gleamed in the bright sunlight as Lillie and her brother climbed to the big double doors.

"I didn't notice you complaining when I suggested it this morning," Lillie said, giving Kellan a sly glance.

Kellan shrugged. "You already know I'm not Xavier or Innis. I prefer books to swords."

"Yes," Lillie said, her shoulders slumping at the mention of their older brothers.

Her first day home and she'd already managed to have a huge fight with Xavier.

Innis was away, patrolling the borders of Southglen with his knight brothers. But Xavier was stationed right here in the city. It had seemed like a great chance to reconnect with him, but that had blown up in her face. And she felt like it was somehow her fault. She was smart. How could she have expected things to change at all in the years she'd been away? Just because she'd grown up didn't mean Xavier wasn't still eight whole years older. And a bit of a prig.

She flushed to herself and shook her head, trying to rid it of the uncharitable thought. Xavier had always looked out for her. That was the important part. So many people were alone in the world. She should strive to remember that when she was ready to push fat-headed family members off a bridge.

"You shouldn't listen that closely to Xavier," Kellan said, guessing the train of her thoughts. "There are plenty of things you can do now that you're home."

"I don't want to do just anything," Lillie said, as they paused outside the library doors. "That's the problem. I want to do something meaningful."

"You can always join Father and I," he said. "What could be more meaningful than researching the Southglen Thrones?"

Kellan pushed through the door into one of the greatest collections of knowledge in the world. The air cooled considerably as they stepped out of the sun, and the sight of books shelved three stories high had always made Lillie feel calm and comforted. So why was her skin tight and itchy now?

"I could…" she said as Kellan started for the front desk.

He paused and glanced at her over his shoulder. His grin turned rueful. "But it's not what you want."

"I'm sorry." She rubbed her hands up and down her arms. "You go ahead. I'll figure something out eventually."

"Of course. I'll meet you back at home, then." Being much wiser than Xavier, Kellan didn't mention that she'd had years at the university to think about what she was going to do with all the power thrumming at her fingertips.

Kellan proceeded to the desk where they held the books Lord Ephyra had requested.

Lillie was already drifting toward her favorite section.

A part of her wished she'd just said yes. Ephyra and Kellan's studies sounded fun. Who wouldn't be interested in the mysterious magic that imbued the Thrones of Southglen? But…it just wasn't the work she wanted to be doing.

Her focus at the university had always revolved around more practical applications of magic rather than theoretical.

She stepped down a row of shelves, running her hand along the spines and stopped when her fingers caught on the worn binding of a big cloth-bound tome. She didn't even have to look at the spine and read the title. She pulled it from the shelf.

"Tales of the Battlemages."

Without paying much attention, she flipped to the middle, to the illustration of a knight in shining plate armor. Beside him stood an impressive figure in swirling robes. Blue fire sprang from his hands, washing over the dark horde that threatened to overwhelm them.

She traced his outline, her fingers as familiar with the feel of the paper as with the sound of her father's voice. How many times had he read this story to her and her brothers?

A sigh escaped her lips.

Research was fun, yes, but her father had raised them all with the ideals of duty and honor. A noble's first obligation was to protect his family. His second, to protect his country.

She was meant for something much more than fun.

Xavier and Innis had already earned their knighthoods. They were off doing important things for Southglen. Why was it so hard to believe she wanted the same thing?

"You can't even talk to strangers without stammering," Xavier's voice rang in her ears. "What makes you think you'll be able to shoot fire at them? Battlemages have nerves of steel. They don't shake when someone says hello. You don't belong on a battlefield, Lillie. You belong home where the rest of us can keep you safe."

Her fingers curled around the worn edges of the book. This had been a mistake. She'd loved these stories while growing up, but now her pleasure in them was soured by the memory of Xavier's scowl, softened only by the way he'd reached out to ruffle her hair. Like she was ten years old again.

She snapped the book shut and slipped it back onto the shelf.

She shouldn't have come. Daydreaming here wouldn't get her any closer to a decision or even a clear path forward. And it wasn't the sanctuary from her brother's words that she'd thought it would be.

She turned on her heel and headed for the door. The thing that irked her the most was that Xavier wasn't wrong. Lillie wasn't outgoing, she wasn't bold. But she still had the same ideals and the same drive as the others. How could she reconcile the two? And more importantly how could she convince Xavier that her competence had nothing to do with her confidence.

Kellan had already collected his books and left. Lillie ignored the concerned look from the librarian at the front desk and pushed out the front door into the sunshine.

Glenhaven had been built into the side of a cliff in an unusual part of the country where the warm air flowed across the plains at the foot of the city, keeping it warm in the winter and cool in the summers. Flowers cascaded over the edges of the different tiers, making it feel like a garden for most of the year.

But Lillie trudged down the steps, eyes on her feet, oblivious to the beauty of the city for once. She'd seen it a thousand times before, and it wasn't nearly as interesting as the worry that circled her head. She was wasting her life and talents. And as much as she loved her family, they weren't doing anything to help her move past that.

The familiar pattern of the marble beneath her feet led her past the market stalls where merchants called out their prices and several inns where the scent of fried meat and battered vegetables made her stomach rumble. But she didn't stop. She trotted up a set of stairs and stopped.

A public garden opened at the edge of the terrace, looking out over the library. Clear water splashed against the blue tiles of a fountain and the breeze wafted through pink and yellow flowers. Ivy draped the entrance, hiding the space unless you already knew it was there.

Lillie pushed through the thick waxy leaves and settled onto the ledge where she could look down across the city. Her favorite spot to think, since she could usually do it alone.

But she'd barely sat when a footstep rang against the marble behind her. She stiffened and her mouth went dry.

Oh, no. Conversation with strangers had never been her thing. Maybe if she just ignored them, they'd think her rude rather than a bumbling bundle of nerves.

She stared at the marble wall and prayed whoever it was would go away.

"I believe my line is, 'hand over your valuables,'" a voice said.

Lillie gasped and whirled.

A man stood in the entryway of the garden. Broad shoulders filled out a linen shirt, and his hair was pulled back from his face in a fashionable tail. He could have been a craftsman or a merchant looking for a place to get away for a moment if it weren't for the smirk on his lips and the dagger in his hands.

Suddenly, Lillie wasn't so worried about making conversation with a stranger. A different sort of fear tightened in her chest.

"W-what?"

The man tilted his head and played with the tip of his dagger. "Come now, you look more clever than that. I said, hand over your valuables."

Lillie swallowed, trying to get rid of the lump in her throat. "What m-makes you think I have any?"

He rolled his eyes. "I do this for a living. I know a good mark when I see one." His gaze traveled down to her feet before raking back up to her face.

Lillie flushed. She'd worn one of her simpler gowns this morning, barely giving it more thought than to make sure it still fit. But the dress was made of fine silk even if it didn't have the gold trim or lace that was currently in fashion.

"Your purse, love." His grin widened. "Or your life. It's usually not a hard choice."

Lillie's jaw ached as she clenched her teeth. "Is my spending money really worth it? I'll have you brought before the Law Throne."

He stalked forward. Lillie tried to skip back, but the low wall of the terrace pressed the backs of her knees. If she retreated any further, she'd plummet to the steps of the library below.

"You know," the thief said as if chatting her up at a party. "It's a lot harder to break the law here, with the princesses looking down at us. But not impossible." He lifted the tip of his dagger and used it to brush a lock of hair from her neck.

Her hands trembled, and she clenched her fists so hard her nails dug into her palms. He was only asking for her purse but there were far worse things she could think of that he could demand. Her tongue stuck to the roof of her mouth.

She could call fire into her hands, just like the battlemages. She could leave this man a dark smear on the marble. She raised her hands to do it. But...

"How do you expect to flame someone if you can't even talk to them?" Xavier's voice said in her memory.

Could she really flame him? Could she do that to another human being? Even one like this? Was her money or her safety really worth another person's life?

She stood there, mouth gaping stupidly as he leaned he blade against her throat and reached for the purse hanging from her belt.

A broad hand landed on the thief's shoulder and wrenched him away. She had a brief impression of shining silver and the color of honey before there was a meaty thud and the thief was clutching his nose. A spray of blood stained the marble at their feet.

"Get your hands off my sister."

"Xavier," Lillie said with a gasp.

Her oldest brother stood so the light glinted from his breastplate and caught his unsheathed sword just right. A woman in an identical breastplate stood beside him. The ivy across the entryway ended in a jagged line. Like someone had cut it.

Xavier spun the thief around, and his grip tightened on his hilt.

"Xavier, no." Lillie held up a hand.

Xavier glared at her.

"You can't just kill him."

He growled under his breath. "Like he was about to kill you?"

"I don't think he really meant that part," Lillie said, her voice losing its strength in the face of his disapproval.

Xavier snorted. "Then you're an idiot."

Lillie's breath escaped through her lips, but she refused to actually cry in front of him. She bit her lip hard enough to hurt.

Xavier sighed like it pained him. "Ashlin, will you take this creep to the Justice Hall?" he said to his partner. "I want to escort my sister home."

"My pleasure," Ashlin said, hauling the thief to his feet. "Don't you know how to pick your battles?" she said as they disappeared through the ivy.

"How was I supposed to know she had a big bwother following her awound." The workman's voice floated back to them. Blood still cascaded from his nose.

Lillie flushed hard enough to make her cheeks sting, and she stared at her feet.

"Let's go," Xavier said.

"I don't need an escort," Lillie said quietly to her boots.

"Clearly you do. You're just lucky I was on patrol in this tier. What would have happened if I wasn't?"

She opened her mouth to say she would have taken care of it. But would she have? She'd stopped. She hadn't done anything to defend herself.

"Xavier, I..."

"It's okay, Lillie." He ran a hand through his long honey-colored hair and gave her a small grin. "You're fine. You don't have to worry. I'll always be here to protect you."

She followed him out of the garden, throat tight with misery. She wasn't fine. She wasn't supposed to be this...this...weak. Not anymore. Her father had said one day she would be strong enough to protect them. But how could she expect to protect her family, let alone Southglen if she couldn't even protect herself?

Lillie hid in her room for the rest of the day and only crept downstairs when Ephyra and Kellan returned for dinner. Xavier still lurked in the front parlor, ready to either lecture her or hold the tide of would-be thieves at bay by himself.

It wasn't that she resented his rescue or his diligence over her safety. She resented the need for both. She was an Ephyra. She was supposed to be able to defend her father and brothers as well as they defended her. She did not grow up reading all those stories about knights and wizards to turn into some damsel in distress.

But all her convictions melted away the moment someone actually tried to speak to her or worse, threatened her.

Xavier already sat at the long table when Lillie slunk into the dining room and slid into her seat. He gave her a sad smile and reached to ruffle her hair, so at least he wasn't planning another lecture in front of their father.

She bit her lip and ducked her head as Ephyra plopped down at the head of the table, a book in his hands.

"You know, I don't bring my work home with me," Xavier said dryly, eying the tome.

Ephyra blinked up at him. "Yes, we would have a problem if you thumped a criminal across the dinner table, wouldn't we? Very well." Ephyra sighed and slid the book onto his lap under the table cloth, where he would likely sneak looks at it later when Xavier was eating.

"A criminal would at least make for a more interesting centerpiece," Kellan said. He reached across to the drooping flowers that decorated the table. "What are these even supposed to be?"

"Orchids from Mistvale," Ephyra said as one of the servants slid serving platters onto the table beside him. "They don't aggravate Lillie's allergies. Though they also don't seem to have made the trip very well."

Lillie twisted her fingers and sent a little revitalizing spell toward the vase, and the blossoms perked up slightly, taking on more purple hues than their previous gray.

"That's better," Xavier said. "You're turning into the lady of the house more and more each day."

She smiled because she knew he meant it as a compliment, but inside, her heart twisted. What if she wanted to be more than the lady of some grand house? No one was stopping her but herself, but she was turning into a bigger barrier than anything.

Ephyra cleared his throat. "Speaking of, what did you find to do all day after the library, Lilliara?"

Lillie felt her cheeks go hot and red. "Nothing," she mumbled, carefully not looking at Xavier. "I just came home."

Ephyra frowned. "Lingering in your room all day isn't good for your mind. You need to get out more. Find things to challenge yourself. Books, experiences, friends your own age with similar interests."

Lillie pushed a green bean around her plate, making patterns in the gravy. Friends were about as elusive as the honorable purpose she sought. Even at the university it had been hard to find anyone willing to carry on both sides of a conversation.

Ephyra's gaze took on that faraway look that said he had an idea. "The Ollerans are holding a soiree tomorrow night. Unfortunately if one of us doesn't go it will be seen as a great insult and could have political ramifications down the road. But taking the time out of my research could disturb the progress we've made so far..."

He raised his eyebrows. Kellan glanced at Lillie and gave her a sympathetic wince.

Like Kellan, she could already see where this was going, and she raised her hands to say no. No parties. It was exactly the type of interaction she was looking to avoid. She hated empty conversation for the sake of conversation. And that was all society was.

"Wonderful," Xavier said, missing the look between Kellan and Lillie. "Send Lilliara. She's the perfect choice to represent our household."

Lillie huffed but then hesitated. She hated to admit it but he was right. She wasn't doing anything else. And she'd been looking for ways to protect her family. This wasn't shooting fireballs or drawing a sword against a thief. But perhaps she could help the rest of the Ephyras in a way that only she could.

She gulped down what she was about to say and forced her lips into a smile. "Of course," she said though her voice sounded wooden. "I-I'd be happy to help, Father."

After all she couldn't do that much damage to her family's reputation as long as she stood quiet and out of the way. Right?

SIX

THE OLLERANS MANOR stood one tier higher than the Ephyras. It was some sort of status symbol. The closer to the palace you were, the higher up the societal food chain.

She had to double check the address three times before walking the short distance because she'd never actually been to their manor, and she would likely forget it again afterward. There were too many interesting spells that crowded to take its place in her memory.

Lillie paused outside the gate and nodded to the Ephyra guardsman who'd accompanied her. "Thank you, Niles. You may go back now if you'd like."

It wasn't considered polite to bring one's own servants to another noble's party. It made you look like a snob. But Xavier hadn't wanted her to make the short walk alone, and she'd only just kept her brother from walking her himself.

Niles touched his helmet. "Thank you, miss. I actually have a girl down the way. I was going to see if she was up for a walk in the moonlight."

"Oh," Lillie said with a surprised smile. "Well, good luck then."

"Thank you, miss. What time will you be needing an escort home?"

Lillie sighed. "I have to stay at least an hour to make a good impression. But not too late. Be back here by ten? Will that be enough time for your walk?"

"I appreciate any time I can steal a moment with her. See you then, miss."

He tipped his helmet again and left her to make her way inside. She stepped through the front door, held open by an ancient butler, and smoothed her gown. She hadn't had any new dresses made since the last time she'd been home, so it wasn't particularly fashionable compared to the other women around her, but it fit well enough. Sort of. It was a little tight across the chest, but at least she was still short. Blessings in disguise and all that. And she was told the green brought out her eyes.

The butler gestured her down the marble hall, and Lillie tried to stay close to the walls, out of the way of the other guests. She tripped over the edge of her skirt and thanked the gods she'd decided to go with slippers instead of the heels some of the other women were wearing. She shuffled the rest of the way into the ballroom, her face flaming.

Inside she couldn't help gasping. The entire room was roofed with glass, giving the party an open-air feeling. As if they stood in a garden instead of a manor.

She gawked, one hand on the column beside her, until a fellow guest in silver brocade knocked into her shoulder and glared at her. She skipped out of the way and ran into a server. His tray clattered to the floor and a wine glass shattered on the marble.

"Oh, I'm so sorry," Lillie said, her hands creeping to her cheeks. "Please, let me help you."

"No need, miss," the server said. His tone was placid enough, but Lillie searched for exasperation or anger under his rigid smile. "Don't hurt yourself. I'll manage this." His hands worked quickly, and he had gloves to protect them from the shards of glass.

She cleared her throat awkwardly and stepped back. If only she knew a spell that would let her melt into the wall. But she'd only taken one illusion class.

"Ah, Miss Ephyra," a voice hailed her from the edge of the dance floor. "Wasn't expecting to see you here. What a delight."

A dandy in blue velvet with cream lace at his wrists made his way through the crowd, and Lillie admired the way he navigated without bumping into any of them. She recognized him as one of Innis's friends.

"Sir Hiddlesworth," she said and gave him a little nod. She might have only been a miss but the Ephyras outranked a mere baronet.

He snatched her hand before she could think to clasp it behind her and bowed low, placing a moist kiss on her knuckles.

"You've certainly grown up," he said, smirking up at her. "I'm not sure you remember me. You used to hang around the practice yard while your brothers whacked me with sticks. You were beautiful then, but now you're possibly the most radiant thing in this room."

"Er, I remember you," she said. Though she wasn't sure bringing up their age difference was a sound tactic. And the rest of his words made her want to crawl out of her skin into something more comfortable.

She squared her shoulders and tried to think of herself as a knight throwing herself in front of an enemy's blade. She was doing this so her family wouldn't have to. That made enduring the outright flirting worth it, right?

"My mother is after me to find someone just like you. Beautiful and accomplished."

She cringed at the obvious line. What did he know about her

accomplishments? They hadn't really spoken since she was five, and two minutes of shallow compliments at the edge of a ball hardly counted as conversation. Would his mother be impressed with Lillie's complete lack of grace and poise? Would she like her son spending time with a woman who studied magic dangerous enough to be classified "restricted?"

Sir Hiddlesworth leaned closer, possibly going for subtlety but coming off more like a tree about to topple. "Would you dance with me?"

Her skin went hot, then cold, and she tried to swallow but her throat was too dry.

"I-I—no thank you," she blurted out around her thick tongue. "I was just…I like the edges of things. The party. I don't really want to be…" She waved her hand at the dancing couples, trying to find words that wouldn't be immediately offensive. "Out in the open."

"Ah, trying to avoid unwanted suitors, eh?" he said, giving her a broad wink. "Like Otis the Odious. It's too bad he had to be here, but I suppose it is his uncle's house."

Lillie snagged a fluted glass from a passing server and quaffed it in one go. The sparkling wine burned on its way down but at least it gave her the edge she needed to smile and make her tongue work. "Yes. It would be impolite to kick him out."

Sir Hiddlesworth took her hand and tucked it into his elbow, oblivious to the way she jumped. "Don't worry. I'll protect you."

"No need," Lillie squeaked. How did she get him to stop touching her? He obviously didn't think he was doing anything wrong but his complete obliviousness made her even more uncomfortable.

"I was just—I was just about to find the ladies' room." Surely he wouldn't follow her in there. Though with the way he couldn't seem to take a hint, she wouldn't be surprised if he tried.

He turned to protest, but she yanked her hand away from his

and darted away through the crowd. Her heart hammered in her chest.

Over her shoulder, she caught a glimpse of Sir Hiddlesworth's baffled look.

She turned her face away and hugged the wall, staying out of the way of the dancing.

What was wrong with her? Why couldn't she stand there and flirt and return compliments the way everyone else in the world did? She wove her way between guests who seemed to actually be enjoying themselves, laughing and dancing and acting like this was a party.

But when someone like Sir Hiddlesworth approached her and started talking nonsense, she froze. Her brain kept racing through thoughts like how insincere it all seemed while the rest of her remained rigid in panic.

An analytical bit of her mind wondered if it was just the men. Maybe she should run an experiment. Would she react the same way if one of the gorgeous women around her paid her compliments and asked her to dance?

The thought made her pause on the edge of the dance floor. But she shook her head and moved on. She didn't know the answer to that. Because in the end, Lillie didn't know what exactly she wanted in a partner or companion. The only thing she did know was that she wanted the space and the time to find out, without all this crowding around trying to win her over nonsense.

A hallway opened on her right, blessedly clear of guests, and she ducked down the dimly lit corridor. Clearly she was supposed to stay out in the bright ballroom under the stars. But there wasn't actually a sign forbidding her from seeking asylum in the darker parts of the manor, so she pressed on. Perhaps she'd be able to find the library and some peace and quiet along with it.

She pushed open the first door on the left and breathed a sigh when she saw book lined shelves. Thank the gods.

She closed the door behind her and leaned against it for a moment, closing her eyes as the silence fell around her.

Peace at last. She could hide here for the rest of her hour and then leave. As long as people saw her coming and going, she would fulfill her duty to her family.

It took her a moment to realize the silence was only relative compared to the dull roar out in the ballroom. A frantic rustling came from further into the room and a deep voice murmured.

Oh dear. She'd stumbled into something awkward again. Her fingers closed on the door handle.

"No!" another voice rose, much higher.

Lillie sucked in a breath. She released the handle and stepped forward to peer around the end of a bookcase.

A lively fire burned in the ornate hearth across from her, illuminating two rich leather sofas and a deep armchair.

And the back of a tall broad figure in a coat pressing someone up against a dark wood sideboard.

The figure shifted as if to adjust his pants, and Lillie caught a glimpse of the young woman he had trapped. Her hair had been pinned up recently but now it straggled into her eyes as if it had been yanked, and she covered her face with both hands to muffle her sobs.

"Please, don't," she whispered, her voice losing strength.

"You really have to stop saying that," the man said, his voice rumbling with mild amusement. "Pretending you have a choice. You work for my uncle. You have to do what I say. It's you're job."

As the man reached for the girl's skirts Lillie caught sight of the white cap and apron tossed carelessly on the floor nearby. The ties were ripped and frayed.

Heat rose in her chest and beat in her cheeks, but this was very different from the panic in the ballroom. Her fists clenched and the power of the world rose at her command and swirled around her, waiting for her word.

She could just turn around and leave like she'd intended. This wasn't her fight.

But this—this bastard was forcing himself on an unwilling woman. Not just any woman. A servant. A girl under his care he was supposed to protect and safeguard as part of his noble duties. A girl who couldn't fight back against him for fear of the repercussions. Servants could never in a million years strike their masters.

But a noble could most definitely strike another noble.

"Stop this," Lillie said, making her voice ring around the small room. She stepped into the firelight, footsteps firm. All her earlier panic had disappeared. "Now."

The man stilled and craned his head around. "This doesn't concern you."

Now with his face illuminated by firelight, she recognized him. Otis Virvalim. Otis the Odious Sir Hiddlesworth had called him. His features would be handsome enough with that proud nose and chiseled jaw if it weren't for the perpetual sneer and the squint that always made him look like he'd stuffed a lemon up his nose.

"I'm making it my concern," Lillie said, willing all his attention on her. The girl was not one of her servants. She really had no right to feel this concern, and there were plenty of nobles who would agree with him that he was only commanding a reasonable service from someone who worked for him.

But Lillie was an Ephyra. Her father had taught her what duty and honor meant, even if Otis's hadn't. And that duty extended far beyond the walls of the Ephyra manor.

Finally, Otis turned, enough to unpin the unfortunate maid. He gave Lillie his full attention.

Lillie dropped her left hand and gestured to the maid to get out while she could. If Otis was distracted with her, he wouldn't stop the maid from escaping.

The girl slid off the sideboard and scuttled sideways. She didn't bother to retrieve her cap and apron. She just hugged her arms around herself and sprinted for the door.

Otis's face twisted, his lip lifting over his teeth as he looked Lillie up and down.

Lillie waited for the panic to rise. She braced herself for the flood of fear and embarrassment that always rose under a stranger's undivided attention.

It never came. The only thing flooding her veins was a driving sort of heat.

Huh. Maybe Xavier was wrong. Maybe it was easier to protect others than it was to protect herself.

Lillie waited for the door to click shut behind her. As soon as it did, she raised her chin. "You'll leave her alone from now on."

He leaned back against the sideboard and crossed his arms, clearly not caring that his trousers sagged.

"You know, you're too pretty to be that much of a stick in the mud," he said.

Her mouth pinched, and as his words and his look sank in, she realized she was now alone in the room with a rapist.

She spun for the door.

Otis darted across the space and slammed his hand against the wood, trapping her. "Now, now. You denied me my fun with her. You must have had something else in mind."

"Get back, you pig," Lillie said.

"No, really it was cleverly done. Drawing my attention to you. So you must want this."

He grabbed her arms, and Lillie squeaked. He shoved her against the nearest book case and fumbled for her skirts.

Lillie struggled, but Otis outweighed her by a good bit and he leaned into her. She screamed, but he slammed his hand against her mouth to muffle her call and gripped her wrists in his other hand.

Her mind whirled, thoughts spinning past. Would anyone even hear her? Where was Xavier now when she actually needed him?

She tried to bring her hands up, but the power that had swirled around her before collapsed, leaving her cold and shivering. The anger that had lent her strength before abandoned her, replaced with nothing but cold dread.

Lillie twisted and Otis grunted in effort to keep her pinned. Spells crowded her mind but none of them broke through the barrier of Xavier's words.

Weak. She was so weak she couldn't even defend herself.

Her eyes snapped open as Otis released her wrists to grope for her skirts.

She was thinking about this all wrong. She wasn't defending herself here. She was defending the servant. She was defending every woman that Otis thought he could take advantage of.

She had the power to change the future. She had the power to make it so he never touched another woman again. She could protect all of those women, right now, in this moment.

Her skin crawled as he dragged his hand up her leg.

"See, you must wa—"

Lillie's paralysis melted away, and she slammed both hands into his chest. The words of a spell leaped from her tongue, the force of her anger and purpose sending sparks through her voice into her hands.

Otis jerked back as flames spouted from Lillie's palms, cascading over his form. Light lit up his wide eyes and open mouth for a moment before he screamed and stumbled back.

The flames outlined his figue, and he dissolved in light and fire until nothing was left of Otis Virvalim but a twisted black corpse on the rug.

Lillie stared at the smoking ruin that had once been a man, a freezing numbness creeping up her limbs. She hadn't expected to kill him. She hadn't really planned her response at all. And now a man was dead.

No, now a rapist was dead.

The fierce surge of satisfaction caught her by surprise, and she lifted her numb hands to her mouth to keep herself from vomiting all over the remains.

She spun, covering her nose.

Oh gods, oh, gods. What was she going to do? She'd just killed a man. Tears ran down her cheeks. She hadn't even noticed them start.

He…he'd touched her and said those awful things, and then she'd just decided and in a flash it was done.

Her throat closed up, and she choked. She stumbled to the fireplace, leaning over to wheeze.

Breathe, she told herself. *Just breathe. Thinking can come in a second. For now, breathe.*

She sucked air in and out and braced her shaking hands on her knees.

The breaths steadied her just a little, and she felt strong enough to straighten. Her father would know what to do. Xavier would protect her, the way he always did.

She wiped her streaming nose and froze.

No. She couldn't go home. There were more ramifications here than a mere "problem."

It wasn't exactly illegal for a noble to kill another noble. Especially not in self-defense. But there were ancient rules surrounding such an execution, the same way there were for everything else in Glenhaven.

The victim's family could challenge the execution. Lillie would have to defend her actions in open combat. If she lived, then her execution would be declared justified. If she died, well, then she was guilty of murder…and her entire family was guilty by association.

The shaking started again.

She couldn't go home. But she couldn't be caught here either. The maid had seen her. They would know who had executed Otis and the Virvalim family would bring her to the Justice Hall and make her fight.

Lord Virvalim would come after her for sure. And Lord Olleran and Otis's cousins as well. All seasoned knights. She'd wanted to be a battlemage, but this? This would be slaughter. She'd never win. She wasn't even sure how she'd found the strength to kill Otis in the first place.

And she couldn't ask Xavier to fight for her. She'd told him over and over she could protect herself and her family. Well, now was the chance to prove it.

This was her problem. And her consequences.

She would not die in the Justice Hall, bringing the Ephyra family down with her. And she would not go crying to her father or older brothers for help.

She had to leave. She had to take her problems and her consequences with her and go. It was the only way to protect the rest of the Ephyras.

And now she was finally old enough and strong enough to do so.

Lillie left what little remained of Otis in the privy. Even shaking with shock she couldn't leave a library so untidy.

She crept through the empty passages away from the crowded

ballroom and found a small door that led out into the garden behind the Olleran manor.

A stone wall surrounded a little orchard that backed up against the cliff, trapping her. But she found a bench to stand on, and from there, she kicked and climbed her way to the top of the wall. The short drop on the other side hurt her knees but didn't break anything, thank the gods.

She paused, hands on the wall and listened. No one cried out from inside. No one raised the alarm, so maybe she'd managed to escape unseen. A minor miracle to be sure. She was starting to regret that she wasn't any good at illusions.

A little alley ran between the garden wall and the next manor over, leading her to the main street. She peered out, then jerked back, her heart beating in her chest.

Niles stood at the gate with a couple of other liveried servants from the other houses. Crap, it must be later than she thought.

A waist high planter ran along the front of the neighboring manor, holding tall, healthy bushes of wisteria and lavender. Lillie dove for the cover of the plants and crawled across the roots, avoiding Niles and his friends. If they saw her, she'd be doomed before she began.

Her nose itched, and she stopped to suppress a sneeze. Blasted allergies. If she was caught now how would she ever explain crawling through the flower beds? And who knew how much time she had before Lord Virvalim went looking for his son?

She crawled another couple of feet, her eyes streaming, but another sneeze crept up on her and took her by surprise.

"Achoo!"

She froze, burying her nose in the crook of her arm and waited to see if Niles and the others came to investigate.

There was a murmur that sounded like, "What was that?" and footsteps.

Lillie held her breath and crept forward as quietly as she could, careful not to rustle the branches above.

Someone parted the leaves behind her, and she scurried out the end of the planter before they could look deeper.

"Must have been an animal," Niles said as Lillie slipped away down the stairs toward the Ephyra manor.

The lights were off. Lord Ephyra liked to get an early night when he was deep in his research. He always did his best work in the morning.

Lillie swallowed and pushed away the thought of her father as she snuck up the steps of the darkened house and slid into her bedroom. Best not to think of any of them right now. Or she'd lose her nerve completely.

She stripped out of her gown with its lingering scent of burnt paper and leather and stuffed it into the deepest corner of her closet. Then she pulled out the simplest outfit she owned. A linen shirt, a simple blue bodice, and a pair of trousers that were tighter than she remembered. And at last she had a use for those boots Innis had gifted her last year.

When she wasn't encumbered by stained skirts, she rushed to her vanity.

She didn't feel right taking any money while she crept away like a thief in the night. But there was some jewelry that was rightfully hers, either gifted to her or passed down specifically to her. That should buy her way out of the city at least.

She dropped a couple of necklaces into her belt pouch and turned to face the rest of the room with a deep breath.

What else would she need? Funny how she'd read all those adventure novels and never noticed what the hero bothered to pack.

Her bookshelf stood against the opposite wall crammed with her collection. Most of them wouldn't be helpful. They were either novels or beginner's books on magic. But she grabbed her spellbook to hang from her belt. As she settled the tome on her hip, a door swung open down the hall.

Lillie jumped, spilling books all over her floor.

Footsteps came toward her door.

Kellan or Xavier. Unless Innis was back early from his border patrol.

Whoever it was, she couldn't let them catch her here. She desperately wanted to tell someone what had happened. She didn't want to just disappear, but they'd try to talk her out of her decision. Or they'd take it from her entirely.

They'd find out what had happened eventually. Virvalim would never keep quiet about her guilt. But as long as she disappeared, her family wouldn't be involved. By tradition, Virvalim couldn't drag them into it. Unless they insisted on involving themselves before she could escape.

She rushed to the window, leaving the books scattered on the floor, and threw open the shutters. They were built for the mild Glenhaven weather and folded all the way back so she could enjoy the balmy breeze and the flowers on her trellis. The ones her father had imported because they didn't make her sneeze.

"Lillie?" Kellan whispered through her door. "Are you in?"

She swung her leg over the windowsill and bit her lip to keep from crying. She would not balk at this. She would not change her mind.

She clambered down the trellis as quietly as she could, but her grip slipped a few feet from the ground, and she fell the rest of the way.

She stood and rubbed her butt, grateful for once for the extra padding she carried around.

Then she darted through the gate before Kellan could hear and come running.

On the tier above, near the Olleran manor, lights flickered

back and forth through the screening greenery, and guards shouted orders through the night air.

Someone had raised the alarm.

Lillie hurried through the city, nearly tripping on the stairs toward the harbor.

A troop of knights clanked down the sidewalk, and she ducked into an alley to avoid them. They might not be after her specifically, but the less people who saw a blonde half elf running through the city the better.

She snuck behind the shops to get to the next flight of steps and froze.

Blast, a quad of guards dressed in Virvalim's house livery guarded the top of the stairs. The Virvalim estate was so bloated with money she wouldn't be surprised if he'd managed to set checkpoints at every staircase up and down the city.

How could she get past? She could just try bluffing her way through. But that would only work if Virvalim hadn't identified her yet.

Just beyond the stairs, one of the city's many waterways burbled placidly, passing unnoticed under the bridge before it cascaded over the drop to the next tier, creating an idyllic waterfall. None of the guards looked down.

Lillie chewed her lip. It was starting to get raw and chapped.

The waterfall was one of the smaller ones branching down through the city. And the channels were all man-made, smooth and curved.

Before she could think too hard about it, Lillie conjured a tiny fireball and tossed it down the street. It exploded against a stone railing in a shower of sparks.

The guards shouted and ran towards the commotion.

Lillie sprinted behind them, plugged her nose, and leaped over the edge into the water.

Gods, that's cold.

She flailed to the surface and sucked in a breath. She wasn't much of a swimmer but her father had at least made sure she knew how to keep her head above water. She just hadn't realized how hard that would be when the water moved fast and her limbs chilled rapidly.

Before she could gasp more than once, the current carried her over the edge of the falls, and she plunged twenty feet to the next level.

Up, she just had to keep her head up.

She struggled to the surface again, but before she could orient herself and catch her breath, she went over the next waterfall.

She gave up trying to control her path downstream and just pointed her feet in the right direction, poking her head above water whenever she could to grab enough air to stay alive.

A frozen eternity later, she hit the bottom, sinking a good ways into the harbor at the base of the city. As soon as she realized she was free of the churning turbulence of the falls, she kicked out and paddled to the surface for the last time.

Luckily she wasn't that far from the docks. And at this time of night, there was no one to see the bedraggled wizard that hauled herself out of the water. Her trembling legs refused to hold her, and she rolled across the pier, leaving a giant puddle on the planks.

She lay there, gasping for several long moments. Lights bobbed along the different tiers of the city but they were all much further above. She doubted any of them would get down here as fast as she had, so she felt safe enough to just stare up at the terraces of the city that used to be her home.

A lump rose in her throat, and she threw her arm over her face to sob into her elbow.

What was she doing? Was she really strong enough to leave everything behind?

For the first time in her life she realized just how alone she was. Without her family, she had no friends. No mentors or teachers or friendly shopkeepers who could help her. Nowhere to go, nowhere to hide. Lilliara Ephyra had lived her life so quietly that no one would remember that tubby girl who used to sit in the corner and read. Even her favorite teachers had forgotten her name on more than one occasion.

The only ones who would miss her were the ones she was so desperately trying to protect. She'd done what she'd wanted. She'd disappeared without a trace. Her father and her bothers would have no idea what had happened to her. At least not yet. And that would keep them safe from Virvalim's wrath. Tradition demanded that she alone pay for her crime unless she decided to call on a champion. And she couldn't call a champion if Virvalim couldn't even find her.

She peeled her arm away from her eyes and blinked up at the city, forcing herself to say goodbye with a cynical eye. Glenhaven was just a place. Her family was the important part and this was the best way she could serve them right now. She should be proud of what she was doing.

Somehow that didn't make it better.

She climbed to her feet and by the time she'd straightened, the tears had stopped.

Barges docked here all the time, carrying goods down the rivers to the city from the great harbors on the coast. Across the wide bridge in front of her, caravans gathered on the plains before setting off on their trade routes.

She could buy her passage on one of those, either on a barge or a wagon until they were far enough from the city that Virvalim couldn't track her movements anymore. And she had enough jewelry to buy their silence with bribes.

That was a thing people did, right?

And wherever her ride stopped next, she'd switch to another route. Another caravan or ship. And so on and so forth, getting further and further away from the problem until at last one day she would feel safe enough to stop.

She'd find a little town or village, somewhere out of the way where her name and title meant nothing, and she'd start a new life there. Magic was about all she was good for. Maybe she could set up as the local wizard. Drive off pests or live secluded in a stone tower.

Or she could find a job as an adventurer. A battlemage like she'd always wanted.

Her spine straightened, and she stared down at her hands.

Killing Otis had been awful. On so many levels. But…but he wasn't alive to assault anyone ever again.

She *could* protect people.

She whispered words of power and let a little bit of fire gather in her fingers, bolstering her resolve and warming her at the same time. Steam rose from her clothes and her spellbook, which had suffered in her plunge from the heights.

Then she tucked the flame away and squared her shoulders. Lilliara Ephyra went in search of a ride.

PART FOUR
TALON

Talon's origin story is best read after *Sparks and Scales*.

SEVEN

THE CHILD SHIVERED beneath a spreading pine tree. Water dripped from the branches to splash the dry needles at his feet. The rain was the only reason he was alive. Otherwise he'd be dead with the rest.

He shoved the thought away. Too much. Too soon. He rocked himself gently, arms around his knees, the way his mother had rocked him when too many people crowded him or too many voices babbled.

There weren't too many people now.

He buried his head against his knees. There were no more tears left. He'd spent them already.

He couldn't remember what happened, even though it was just a few hours ago. All he remembered was fighting with his mother over something silly. Something about the pretty ribbons she didn't want him to wear.

He'd stamped his feet and screamed. Screaming had never worked before, but he didn't have words for the feeling that tightened in his chest whenever she she told him boys didn't play with dolls or ribbons.

Then someone else was screaming and there was cursing and noise and heat. His mother's face had gone white, and he'd fallen silent in the face of her terror. She pushed him under one of their wagons.

"Hide there," she'd said. "I'll come for you when it's safe."

It was the last thing she'd said to him.

Then the bad men had come, and he'd hidden his face in the dirt for a long time. Until the fire had raged, and he'd thought he would burn under the wagon.

When the rain finally smothered the flames and the world fell still, he knew his mother wasn't coming back.

He'd made it as far as the tree before the shaking started, and he couldn't stand anymore.

The smell of smoke tickled his nose, and he shivered again as a trickle of rain slipped under his collar.

He missed being warm and dry. His father had always kept them warm and dry and fed. The lump in his throat nearly choked him, but he swallowed down more tears.

He had to find someplace to sleep. Something to eat.

He could concentrate on that, those simple tasks. He stood, using the tree trunk to steady his small frame while dried pine needles crunched and slid under his feet.

He trudged, forgetting to look up and around more often than not. But as the sky above the trees grew dim, he caught sight of a rock shelf and remembered camping away from the caravan with his father. They'd used a site like this.

He slid and skid down the hill under the overhang, skinning his hands and knees before he tumbled into the cool, dry cave underneath. Someone or something had dug into the soft dirt at the base and hollowed out an area big enough to feel cozy and safe.

The child curled into himself and slept, too tired to worry about a fire or food.

A wet snuffle woke him a few hours later, and he sat up. Shadows slunk between him and the opening of the cave, long and low. His heart beat in his throat, and he drew his knees to his chest but he didn't cry out or scream. What if the bad men had come back? What if they'd found him?

The largest shadow crept closer, sniffling, and the child realized it was a big black wolf with gray around its muzzle.

The wolf sniffed at his hair and torn clothes and snorted. Then it cocked its head.

What are you doing here, human cub?

It wasn't a voice. More like the hand gestures the caravaners used when communicating from one end of the caravan to the other. But the child realized he could read the words in the tilt of the wolf's head and ears.

He shook his head and tried to shrink deeper into the back of the cave. "I'm lost," he managed to say, voice hoarse from the smoke.

Where is your pack? the big wolf said.

The child shook his head. He still couldn't think about it. Couldn't concentrate on the images of blood and smoke that swirled just out of his reach.

The big black wolf stared at him a moment longer with gold eyes before it huffed. Then it stepped forward and nudged the child with its nose.

Lay down, cub, the gesture seemed to say.

And the child lay down, too spent to be afraid. The wolf curled up around him and others padded forward to join them. One red-brown. One gray. Another brindled. A whole pack surrounded him, laying in a heap, sharing their warmth and the comfort of their presence.

And the child slept deeply.

For weeks, months, and years the wolves shared their cave with him. And when he was strong enough to venture into the filtered sunlight of the forest, they taught him to hunt as they did, with cunning and perseverance.

He grew stronger, until he could keep up with them.

They never took him back to the dead caravan.

But they took care of him the same way his parents had. They kept him warm and dry and fed. They brought him things. Clothes from a broken crate they'd found. A jacket stolen from a wash line. A bow and a quiver from a hunter who'd fallen from a cliff.

They talked to him and he talked back and eventually he learned to talk to them over distances. They didn't use his name, and he was content to forget it. It had never really fit, anyway, and it belonged to that other life. That mother and father who were gone now.

The wolves accepted him no matter what he was called. And they didn't name themselves the way humans did. They named each other for how they were related. Sister, Mother, Brother. The big black wolf was Father to them all.

They called him Cub. And Hunter. And Friend. And that was enough for him.

The hunter knelt in the snow beside the corpse of a wolf. This one had been known as Nuisance to the rest of the pack. He'd been someone's brother or cub, too, but his flighty personality had made even the most loving of family snap at him and label him a troublemaker.

He wouldn't be playing any more tricks or pranks.

The hunter touched the arrow shaft protruding from the wolf's side. Nuisance must have been shot closer to the human village at the end of the valley and still had enough energy to escape before he died. Otherwise the human hunters would have retrieved their arrow. They would have skinned the wolf and hung the rest of him up outside their wall to warn away the rest of the pack.

A big black wolf with sleek shining fur panted beside the hunter.

It's the humans, isn't it? Brother said.

"Yes," the hunter said. He grabbed his bow out of the snow and slung it over his back.

Why do they hunt us? We only seek to feed ourselves the way they do.

"The sheep in the barns and behind gates. They think they belong to the village. They get angry when we eat them."

Father padded up beside the hunter on his other side.

We have little choice, he said. *When the humans take all the deer and the sheep, too.*

"The pack can't move?" the hunter said.

Normally, yes. But we are surrounded with mountains and cliffs on two sides, the human village at the one end of the valley, and another pack at the other. We can't leave without risking a fight with one or the other or braving the perils of the high passes.

"Then we will have to learn to share the valley," the hunter said.

We are trying, Father said. *We are not the problem.*

Father turned and pushed his way through the snow, his big paws leaving divots in the drifts. The other big black wolf known as Brother followed.

The hunter paused for a moment and then mounded the fresh snow across Nuisance. He might have been annoying but he was still pack.

Father waited at the edge of the trees where they could just see the smoke rising from the human village.

We need someone to speak for us, Father said as the hunter joined them again. *Someone whose teeth do not scare them.*

The hunter snorted.

You will convince them, Father said.

"What?" The hunter froze, snow trickling into his second-hand boots.

As much as you have been loved by the pack and raised by us, you are still human. They are more likely to listen to you.

Father rose from his haunches and trotted through the trees, back toward where they'd left the rest of the pack. *Let us know when you are done.*

"That's it, then?" The hunter planted his fists on his hips. "Just, 'see you later?'"

Brother shook the snow from his ruff. *Father has never beaten around the bush.*

"He could have at least said good luck," the hunter grumbled.

You don't need luck. You have the human language. They will listen to you. Brother stepped forward and licked the hunter's chapped knuckles. *What's wrong?*

"Well…" The hunter rubbed his neck. "I haven't spoken to a lot of humans in the last few years, believe it or not."

Brother tilted his head. *Running around the woods with a bunch of wolves will do that to you.*

The hunter snorted as Brother leaped from one snow bank to the next.

Come on, Brother said. *Or don't you want to get this over with?*

The hunter sighed and followed.

The human settlement sat tucked against the mountain on the west side of the valley with the snowy meadows and forest stretched out in front of it.

The hunter's nose wrinkled as they got closer to the gates. He'd hated the smell of woodsmoke ever since…ever since he'd lived with the wolves. Especially when it was damp, and the village was rife with it.

"Stay close," the hunter told Brother. "I don't want them getting the wrong idea about you."

What? That I'm a wolf? I think that's the right idea.

The gate stood open, but a couple human hunters guarded the rough wooden palisade, their weapons in their hands.

The hunter raised a hand in cautious greeting.

The humans glanced between him and the big black wolf, but finally they waved him through.

"Looking for someone specific, boy?" the nearest one asked as he passed. The man didn't seem unfriendly. The squirm in the hunter's gut had to be his own nerves.

"I'm just—just looking for someone in charge to talk to," he said. There. Had that come out too much like a wolf? He never had to worry how growly his voice was with the pack. Half the time he didn't even need to speak out loud with them so it tended to be rusty with disuse.

The man didn't seem to mind. He wiped his red nose and pointed to a fenced in area directly in the middle of the village. Little houses with thatched roofs surrounded the clear space.

"The elders meet on the green around noontime. You won't have long to wait. If you'd like, there's a pot of something hot to drink set up by the smithy. You're welcome to pour yourself some."

The hunter dug deep for manners his mother had taught him long, long ago. "Thank you," he said.

"You're welcome, boy."

The hunter flinched, and the man eyed him. But the hunter escaped into the village without another exchange.

Brother stuck close to the hunter's side. A couple of women in thick winter skirts and shawls wrapped around their shoulders goggled at the big black wolf and skipped aside to let them pass.

The smithy rang with the sounds of hammer and anvil so the communal pot wasn't hard to find. A middle aged woman stirred it, her chapped hands steady on the ladle.

The hunter held out a battered cup he'd found in a burnt out shack beside the river last summer. He didn't mind sticking his face in ponds and streams like the wolves did, but sometimes it was nice to be able to carry a cup of water somewhere.

The woman smiled, revealing crooked teeth, and she ladled something dark and hot into his cup.

"There you are, young man."

The hunter's chest tightened, and he coughed. Why did his cheeks burn and his hands shake? He steadied them on the cup and bobbed his head in thanks before he escaped.

What's wrong? Brother said, pressing against his side as they walked.

"I don't know," the hunter whispered. "I just...don't feel right."

Are you sick? The wolf said. *I can find a spot for you to drag your butt if you need to.*

The hunter grimaced. "Ew, no. Not like that. It's just...It's when they talk to me. There's something not right. Like I don't fit what they're seeing."

Well, I've always thought you were more wolf than human on the inside. Maybe they're only seeing the human.

"Maybe," the hunter said. "At least that's close."

He'd felt this before in that long ago time before the wolves. He'd been different then, too. But different how? If he could just put a name to it maybe that would make it better.

Maybe Brother was right. The walls of the settlement leaned in a little, feeling like the edges of of a cage. Maybe he'd lived too much of his life running in the open to feel comfortable inside walls.

He shook his head and made his way to the open space the gate guard had indicated. The village green was hemmed in by a rough log fence. A circle of stumps provided basic seating, and the hunter plopped down on one, cradling his tin cup in his hands, preserving the heat.

No one had gathered on the green yet except for one ancient woman who hunched over her knitting. Her gnarled hands moved with surprising grace and skill, fingers flashing in and out despite the half gloves covering her palms.

She gave the hunter a grin wide enough to split the seams of her face.

"Haven't seen you before," she said. "What's your name?"

Her smile invited him to grin as well even though the squirm in his gut intensified.

"Um, I don't...I don't really have one," he said.

She tilted her head, attention on him, but her knitting didn't even slow. "Everyone calls themselves something."

"The wolves call me the Hunter," he said, glancing at his companion, who'd curled up at his feet, keeping them warm. "And I call him Brother." Except the word came out sounding like a growl and a bark.

Her needles paused for a second before resuming. "They talk to you," she said, eyebrows raised in surprise.

"I...guess so," he said. Deep down he'd known that was unusual, but he'd been so little when they'd found him that it hadn't really registered. His lips pressed thin. Great. Another thing to make him different.

"You don't need to look like you've stuck a lemon up your butt."

That surprised a laugh out of him. "What?"

"So sour. Nature magic is a gift from the gods."

"I don't know that it's really magic."

"Why not? I know some spell casters up in the hills who talk to their animals. And rangers can work with the land and its creatures."

The hunter barely knew what magic was, let alone how to cast spells. That certainly didn't fit. But talking to the wolves felt so natural, and he'd always been able to find water and game.

"Maybe," the hunter said reluctantly.

The woman didn't seem put off by his reticence. "I'm Nan," she said. "Least that's what everyone's called me so long it's stuck. So what do the wolves want?"

The hunter's mouth dropped open.

"Oh, don't look like that. It weren't hard to figure. A stranger comes in with a great big beast like yours tame as kitten, claiming to talk to the pack. Clearly you're with them. And it's been a hard winter on all of us, so I'm sure they want something."

"That's…true. The wolves are just trying to survive. I've steered them away from the sheep as much as I can, but still the human hunters here kill us. I mean them." He gestured back toward the gate and the armed guards.

"The hunters think it's their duty to protect us," Nan said. "From wolves and bandits alike. If the wolves stray too close, they're going to feel threatened."

The hunter shook his head. "We're not threatening anyone. At least we're trying not to. But with the hunters taking all the game in the valley, the wolves have to range further and further to hunt for themselves."

"Can't they find new hunting grounds?"

The hunter raised his chin. "This is their home, too. Besides, they can't make it over the passes in the mountains, the village blocks this end of the valley, and there's another pack that's claimed the territory at the other end. We risk violence and death on all sides."

"I see."

Several villagers drifted onto the green and took places on the stumps around them. The hunter sat back, biting his tongue. He'd have the chance to argue his case, and Nan had been kind so far. She wasn't the one to take his frustration out on.

A man in fur-lined gloves and a wraparound coat took his place in the center of the circle. "All right, let's do this quickly.

Even we don't have enough hot air to stay warm out here for long."

The gathered villagers chuckled. The hunter's fingers tensed on his cup, rehearsing his words in his head.

"Nan, you want to get us started?"

The hunter whipped around to focus on Nan, who creaked to her feet.

She stood and cracked her back. "I'll keep talking as long as you all keep listening to me. We have a request from the wolf pack of the valley." She gestured to the hunter.

The hunter swallowed as all their eyes focused on him.

A man across the circle snorted, making his frost covered beard ripple. "What could a bunch of wolves have to say?"

"'Stop killing us' was the gist of it, I believe," Nan said, raising an eyebrow. "Right?"

The hunter nodded. "That's about it."

The man with the beard scowled. "Maybe they should learn to stay further away."

"Maybe we should learn to work with them," Nan said.

The hunter started.

"This is Lod, our lead huntsman." Nan gestured to the bearded man. "Lod, what was the complaint you were going to bring to the elders today?"

Lod crossed his arms, breath huffing between his lips like a cloud. "The huntsmen are spread too thin. Between the bandits we have to fend off and the wolves, we hardly have time to keep the village fed. And that's our first priority normally."

Nan tapped her teeth. "Hunter, can you see a way to work together on this?"

The hunter opened his mouth and hesitated. It would never work, would it? The humans would never trust the pack. But Nan stood there handing him the answer and all he had to do was grab it and run.

"We could make a deal," he said. That was a thing humans did. It's what his parents had done all the time. "The wolves will patrol the valley and keep the bandits away, if the village promises to stop killing them and…and pays them."

Lod looked like he was about to scoff again, but instead he paused a moment to think. "What would they want for helping us?"

"Game," the hunter said immediately. He glanced down at Brother. "If you provide a buck a week or a couple of sheep every now and then, the wolves will have enough time to hunt the bandits. And if you're not hunting bandits or wolves you'll have enough time to hunt game."

"The wolves can't eat the bandits?" someone muttered, but Nan glared them into silence.

"Lod?" Nan said. "Is this acceptable?"

The huntsman ran his hands over his face and beard. "We'd have to trust wild animals."

"Not so wild," Nan said, glancing at Brother. "You've worked with rangers before."

"Gods help us, but it makes sense," Lod said, dropping his hands. "Very well. It's a deal."

The hunter's chest swelled, and he held his breath a moment to make sure it was all real. Had he really just helped? He'd argued and they'd listened.

Nan shuffled across the green to him. "Don't look so surprised. Words matter, kid." She handed him a pair of fingerless gloves made from a bright purple yarn. The ones she'd been knitting as they talked. "Those are for you. But feel free to come back and trade other things, too. Wolves are good company, sure, but maybe you want some friends with less teeth sometimes."

The hunter shifted the pack on his back and followed the stream, which was swollen with snow melt.

Brother trotted beside him, leaving big paw prints in the muddy bank. The black wolf stopped twice to look over his shoulder, back at the woods they'd left behind.

"What is it?" the hunter said.

Brother shivered, his hackles settling. *I don't know. I just don't feel right leaving the pack today.*

The hunter tilted his head. "Why? We've left them dozens of times this winter. It's always been fine."

It just feels different today. Can we hurry?

"Sure," the hunter said. "Nan said she'd meet us on the green and we don't have any other business."

He picked up his pace and headed for the bridge near the human village. Normally he'd just hop across the stream, but with the banks flooded for spring, he didn't quite dare.

The guards at the gates greeted him with smiles. "Good hunting, boy?" one of them asked.

The hunter tried to smile back. "Good enough," he said and hurried past them, Brother on his heels.

Nan waited on the green, tubs of wash water at her feet. It was warm enough she'd rolled up her sleeves to scrub the winter grime from her blankets and sheets.

"Ho, Hunter," she said. "What have you brought us today?"

The hunter slung his pack to the ground, avoiding the biggest puddles of mud and flipped open the top. A variety of weapons lay inside. Some were good quality but most were cobbled together out of sharpened metal plates tied to rough clubs.

"Hmm," Nan said. "You'd think with winter being over the bandits would be a bit less desperate and a little more organized."

"I think it's taking them longer to recover than it took you. These were scrawnier than usual and didn't put up much of a fight. I counted fifteen."

Nan raised her eyebrows and sank back on her heels. "Your pack took on fifteen? I'm impressed." She eyed him up and down.

The hunter flushed and shrugged. "They listen when I tell them how and when to attack…"

"And?" Nan said, guessing there was more.

"I can hear the land. Like you were talking about. And it responds."

Nan smirked. "Told you you're a ranger. I take it you've been practicing?"

The hunter's lip twitched, and he held a hand over the soft ground. A vine surged up through the mud, swaying in the slight breeze before it wrapped gently around Nan's wrist.

"Well, look at that." Her eyes shone as she stared. "You're learning to listen to it."

She shook her hand and the hunter let the vine collapse with a word.

"I love it when I'm right," she said.

The hunter snorted. "I'll bet."

Nan kicked the side of the pack. "These are worth a buck and a sheep. I'll have Lod haul them out to the normal place for your pack to retrieve. And tell them thank you."

"You're welcome," the hunter said.

"I've laid some things aside I thought you could use. That coat you're wearing is nothing but patches now, and I think I found one in your size. And there's a nice new knife if you think you want it."

The hunter perked up. "I loved the last one you gave me."

"Sure thing. Helen, would you grab the goods from the smithy?" Nan asked one of the other village women.

Helen straightened and dried her hands on her apron. "Of course." She returned a moment later with a dagger the length of her arm and a new coat. "Here you are, young man."

The hunter flinched and just managed to take the things without fumbling. He mumbled his thanks and backed up a step.

Helen didn't seem to notice, returning to her work without comment. But Nan speared him with a glance.

"You've been welcome here for months," she said quietly. "Why are you still so skittish around us? Do you distrust all humans or just us?"

The hunter shook his head. "No. It's not…not trust."

"Then what is it?"

"I'm not sure I can explain."

Nan turned over an empty washbasin right there in the mud and plopped down on it like she had all the time in the world. "Try," she said.

The hunter scratched at the patchy beard on his chin. It had gotten thicker every winter for a couple years and his old knife wasn't sharp enough to shave it down now.

"I don't even know that I have the words for it." But that wasn't exactly true. He'd spent most of the winter trying to place his feelings every time he came into the village. The wolves didn't help. They felt things and moved on. They didn't get stuck in the sinking pool of discontent. Like spring mud that just wouldn't let go.

"I feel like everyone here looks at me and sees something I'm not. They see something different than I do when I think about myself."

"Do you think of yourself as a wolf?"

The hunter shook his head. "It's not that. It's…deeper than that somehow. And more specific."

She raised an eyebrow. Waiting.

The hunter blew out a breath. His tongue stuck to the roof of his mouth. The last time he'd voiced anything close to this, he'd been too small to know better. And it had made his mother sad.

"I don't like it when people call me 'boy.' Or 'young man.' It's just…not quite right."

Nan didn't say anything. Which was better than running away screaming. Or getting that white face, pinch-lipped look that made his insides squirm.

"The wolves, they always called me Cub or Hunter. Never Brother or Sister. I think because they know that neither fit."

The hunter smoothed a seam on the new jacket, not meeting her eyes.

"That's hard," she said without having to think about it. "It makes you different. People count on what they can see to tell them about the person underneath."

The hunter flinched. "Great," he said.

Nan held up a hand. "I didn't say it made you wrong. Just different. And the outside doesn't match the inside for a lot of people. It's just not usually so drastic. People look at me and see a doddering old woman whose mind is probably going."

"And they'd be wrong," the hunter said with a grin.

"Dead wrong. And it's their fault they made the assumption. But that's not going to stop them from making the same mistake with everyone they meet. We're creatures of habit."

"So, there's nothing I can do."

"There's nothing you *have* to do." Nan wrapped her knuckles on his knee. "Not your job to change their thinking. That's up to them."

"So, I just have to ignore it."

Nan shrugged. "Or grow strong enough that it doesn't bother you anymore."

"Because that sounds so easy."

"Didn't say it would be, Hunter. It's also not fair, which you haven't pointed out yet, but I'm sure you were getting to."

The hunter rubbed the back of his neck. "I'm not sure I like the human world."

"You can't tell me wolves don't have gender. I know your friend there is male." She gestured to Brother.

"They do," the hunter said. "They just don't use it or abuse it the way humans do. It's not…important in the same way. And they might have the right of it. This whole thing makes me want to run back to the woods and hide. At least there I don't always feel looked at. Examined and judged to be different or wrong."

Nan regarded him for a moment before she stood and shuffled to the clothesline strung across the village green. Her deft fingers shuffled through the linens hung there until she came to a long drape of black fabric. She took it down and tossed it to him.

"No retreating," she said. "You're out of the woods now. Sure you can go back in and not come out if you really want. But you don't have to. And I don't think it's good for you. You've grown so much in the last few months, interacting with your own kind. But you can still hide. If that's what it takes to make you feel safe. If that's what it takes to keep growing, keep getting stronger, you can hide yourself. At least until you know what face you want to force the world to accept."

The hunter spread the damp folds of cloth to find a cloak with a deep hood. He'd be able to pull it low over his face, keeping it in shadow no matter what the weather.

His fingers stroked the tight weave. None of the other villagers felt the need to hide. Half of them didn't even wear hats anymore now that the air had warmed up.

It was a step. Maybe in the right direction. Maybe not. But it was a step either way. A decision he'd have to make.

A declaration that he was different. If only to himself.

He didn't remember his mother's face anymore. But he could remember her tight lips. The way her eyes had gone confused and unhappy.

"Maybe," the hunter said, but he couldn't keep the reluctance out of his voice.

She didn't make him explain it this time. "I'll keep it for you," she said. "You can decide later if you like."

"Thank you, Nan," he said quietly, handing the cloak back to her.

"Don't thank me. It just means I'm forcing you to visit me again."

He grinned as he stood. "Clever. I'd better go. I promised Brother we wouldn't stay so long."

She turned back to her washing. "Remember what I said. You'd better be back to visit before too long."

Brother surged to his feet and shook himself before following the hunter back out into the wilds. The hunter kept his head down to avoid goodbyes from the villagers. Most of them were used to him by now, but some still tried to waylay him and get him to talk. And they were never as soothing as Nan.

Maybe she was right. Maybe he did need a way to hide from the world without retreating entirely. Would wearing a hood make it easier to talk to people? Maybe it would feel like carrying the forest around with him.

He shook his head as they crossed the bridge and plunged back into the trees. He already had a hard time fitting in with the villagers. If he wore a hood all the time, he'd just have to explain that instead of himself.

An hour later, he still wasn't closer to deciding, but they should have been getting closer to the pack. He lifted his nose to the wind. The wolves had been moving dens up near the north end of the valley.

He couldn't smell them yet.

The hunter stopped to listen. "Do you hear them?"

Brother's ears twitched to and fro and his nostrils flared. *I do not.*

There was something else though. A low whooshing sound far

off but getting closer. It sent a shiver down the back of his neck and he realized if he'd had hackles they would have been raised.

He didn't recognize the noise and these were *his* woods. He should have recognized everything in here.

The hunter pulled his bow from his back and turned just as a massive shape blotted the sun, casting a shadow over a good section of the forest.

"What the—"

A roar rang through the trees, and the hunter clapped his hands over his ears as the sound ricocheted off the nearest peaks. Brother whimpered and pawed at his head.

The shape swooped low and the trees rocked, showering the forest floor with leaves and pine needles.

The hunter threw himself to the side, behind a trunk, as a column of fire poured out of the sky.

Brother dove beside him, cowering. The hunter threw his arms around the wolf to shield him from the heat, but the fire crackled up the trunks, racing through the spring-damp undergrowth as if it was dry kindling.

The massive shape beat scaly wings, fanning the flames. It raised its snout to roar again, then swept away across the valley.

Heat made the hunter's skin tighten and ache, but he sprang to his feet and darted to an outcrop of rock where the flames hadn't reached to squint at the retreating monster.

"Was that...was that a dragon?"

Who cares what it was? Brother said, circling his legs. *It tried to kill us.*

"Shit. The entire valley is on fire."

The entire valley... Brother whined looking out over the flaming trees. Cinders fell through the air like snow.

"The pack," the hunter whispered.

They turned as one and dashed through the flames. The dragon fire had burned fast enough that it was already retreating from a lot of the spring-damp forest, leaving a trail of blackened trunks and foliage in its wake.

Brother and the hunter sprinted through the burnt trees to the new den.

But the pack wasn't there. They exchanged a worried look and traced the path the pack would had taken.

Over a ridge the hunter stumbled to a halt, mouth falling open. Spread on the downhill slope, a black swathe covered what had been verdant land just that morning. The hunter recognized the peaceful glen, but now it was blackened, darkness climbing the trees until they spread thin empty branches across the sky.

Brother whimpered and slunk closer.

A wolf's corpse lay smoking just at the edge of the black.

The hunter knelt. He could barely recognize Father by his grizzled muzzle. The old wolf looked like he'd been caught in a blast by the dragon.

It was hard to tell with so much of the world burning, but this spot…this black spot was different. The trees weren't charred, they were just dead as if all the life and color had been sucked out of them.

The hunter held a hand over the blackened ground and tried to call forth a vine. Nothing happened.

The dragon? Brother said, ears laid flat against his skull.

"I don't know what else it could be. But this place isn't burned. It's just…dead."

Whatever it did, it killed Father.

"Yes," the hunter laid a hand on the old wolf's head, fighting against the choking feeling in his throat. It was so similar. The smell of damp burning wood. The grief and loss.

"The pack. They have to be around somewhere. They wouldn't have tried to escape the valley without Father." They'd be scattered without his leadership.

Brother searched. All up and down the valley he sniffed,

following the wolves' trail. The hunter followed close, looking for evidence of their passing. Tufts of fur, prints, the scent of fear.

Nothing.

Nothing except three more dead spots and swathes of fire blackened forest crossing what little traces of the wolves they could find.

At last, exhausted and shaking, they stopped at the edge of the southern forest. Brother raised his head to howl, calling for their family one last time.

The forest smoldered under the moonlight, but the air was still and silent. No one answered his call.

EIGHT

TWO DAYS after they'd visited with Nan, Brother and the hunter stumbled back up the valley to the human village. Black smoke billowed into the sky though it seemed like most of the fires had been put out. The rough wood palisade tumbled on the side facing the woods, charred until it had crumbled under its own weight, and many of the thatched roofs still smoldered.

Figures dragged bodies to the village green, laying them out in neat rows. The process was strangely quiet, the remaining villagers hollow-eyed and close-mouthed as if they'd already done their weeping.

Lod greeted the hunter at the edge of the green, taking in his soot-stained clothes and shaking hands.

"You too?" the huntsman said quietly.

The hunter just stared, eyes burning. They hadn't stopped burning. "I can't find the pack. I don't know…I don't think they made it."

Lod ran a hand through his hair, leaving bits standing on end, stained dark with soot. "If they faced what we faced, there might not be anything left."

Too many houses smoldered nearby. Too many bodies lay on the green.

A familiar figure was tucked beside the fence. Someone had crossed her arms over her chest.

The hunter's throat went thick and tight as he knelt beside Nan. He wanted nothing more than to throw his head back and howl his grief like Brother. But no sound made it past the tightness in his chest. No howl, not even a whimper.

"She wasn't running," Lod said behind him. "She was making sure everyone got out okay."

"But not everyone did."

"No. It's funny. She was the same age as my grandma. But I always thought she would outlive me."

Lod pulled a long piece of black fabric from the fence where it had hung. "She left this for you. Said you'd come back for it if you wanted it."

The hunter took the cloak between his hands. Even with her laying there still and silent he couldn't imagine a future without Nan chiding him, pushing him, asking him to visit her.

He slung the cloak around his shoulders and fastened it. He'd wear it as a tribute to her kindness and wisdom. It hurt to look at, to remember, but he relished that pain right now. It felt better than the numbness.

Brother sat beside the gate to the green, head bowed, panting. The hunter wasn't sure what the wolf was feeling, but if it was the same emptiness, then he would let him be. The hollowness rang inside the hunter's head, begging to be filled with something, anything.

"What now?" he said mostly to himself. How many times could you lose a family and start over? How many times could you stand back up after that?

"I sent Markus to track the dragon," Lod said, voice growing firmer. "He came back this morning with the news.

The beast is holed up in the north mountains. I don't want to risk the entire village, but we can't stay here if that thing is going to come raiding every time it's hungry. We're going after it."

Lod leaned on the fence and focused on the hunter. "We could use a man with experience in the woods and tracking down monsters. You want to come?"

Blood pounded in the hunter's ears. It surged under his skin, making him feel itchy and antsy. The missing howls of the pack rang around the emptiness in his head and heart. He could fill that emptiness with something. He could fill it with anger, with rage. And he could direct those at something that deserved it. The dragon would never take another family. It would never burn down another village, or strike down an old woman before her wisdom had changed the world.

He took a breath and his chest swelled. The acrid smoke lit up familiar memories of pain and fear. But this time…this time there was something he could do about it.

"Yes," the hunter said. "Yes, count us in."

They left the next morning when the sky was still gray and the air clear and chilly. The hunter wrapped Nan's cloak tight around his shoulders, but he didn't pull the hood up. Not yet. It seemed like an admission, and he wasn't ready to admit anything to himself or to the other huntsmen yet. And it seemed silly to try to hide any part of himself when they were trekking up the side of a mountain to confront a dragon.

No one in their little valley had ever hunted such big game before. Even basilisks and rock wyrms were scarce here. Lod claimed he'd slaughtered a tunnel drake once, but it had been long ago.

Brother stuck close to the hunter's legs as they trudged through the forest and made their way into the foothills.

Why are we going toward the big scary thing that wants to eat us? he said. *We should be running away. This is stupid.*

"What else are we supposed to do?" the hunter asked. "We can't let it kill anyone else. You saw what it did to the forest. Not just the burning but those dead spots, too."

We can move, Brother said. *We can sneak through the other pack's territory at the end of the valley. We can leave. We don't have to fight.*

The hunter scowled as he picked his way up the goat trail the huntsmen were following. "Don't you want to fight? Aren't you angry? This thing killed all of them. It killed Father, and it killed our brothers and sisters and the cubs."

And now we don't have a pack, Brother said. *A wolf without a pack should run away. He has no one to guard his back.*

"I'm not running," the hunter snapped. "I want to do something. I *have* to do something."

Brother whined, but he didn't turn around and go back. He padded along with his head down.

Clearly the wolf didn't feel the same burning ache in his chest. He didn't feel the tingle in his legs that called him on, further and further up the mountain to where the threat lay. How could he not feel the anger simmering under his skin?

Lod climbed just behind them, bringing up the rear of the party. He gave the hunter a look, and the hunter realized he'd spoken out loud to the big wolf. He flushed.

"Different opinions?" Lod said.

The hunter blew out his breath. "Wolves don't confront bigger predators unless they have the whole pack to back them up."

"Smart." Lod squinted up the trail. "Maybe smarter than we are right now."

The hunter shook his head. "But we have to do this. The valley won't be safe again until that beast is dead."

"True. It's necessary. But that doesn't make it smart. If we all wanted to live, we'd leave the valley. But then plenty of us would die out there trying to make new homes for ourselves, so..." Lod shrugged.

The hunter frowned at his boots. The trail wound up the side of a peak, disappearing around a bend ahead of them.

"Nan, said you could speak to them," Lod said, jerking his chin at Brother who trotted tirelessly upward, body low and ready, eyes alert. "Can you talk to all animals?"

"Only the ones who listen," the hunter said. "Most don't want to have anything to do with humans or wolves."

"So you're screwed on both sides."

The hunter huffed a laugh. "Yeah." Ahead of them the first of the huntsmen disappeared around the bend in the trail, placing their feet carefully since it got narrow here.

"Do you think you can talk to the dragon?"

The hunter was surprised enough to stop dead in his tracks and stare back at Lod. Lod just returned his look placidly.

The hunter's brows drew down, and he spun to continue climbing. "I'm not talking to the beast that slew my family."

"Fair enough," Lod said behind him. "I'm just looking for ways to be smarter about this."

The hunter hugged his elbows, concentrating on his footing. At the bend he straightened and flattened himself against the cliff face and shuffled around the corner.

"Nan called you Hunter," Lod said, following. Brother picked his own way across the treacherous path. "Is that your name?"

This was more conversation than the hunter had had with one human being in his entire adult life. Except for Nan, but she'd always had a way of talking without expecting anything in return.

"I have no name," the hunter said.

"Everyone needs a name, boy."

"Well, it's definitely not 'boy,'" the hunter snapped.

Lod was quiet a moment. "I'm sorry. You're right. It's patronizing. It's just, you remind me of my son."

The hunter took a steady breath and unclenched his jaw. "I didn't know you had a son."

"He died three days ago when the dragon struck."

The hunter stepped onto a wider part of the path and paused long enough to meet Lod's eyes.

"I'm sorry," he said.

Lod nodded, lips pulled in a sad smile. He gestured the hunter on.

"You can always pick one, you know," he said behind the hunter's shoulders. "A name. Not having one already can be a blessing that way. You can pick something that fits you."

The hunter was so fixed on Lod's words he didn't notice the man in front of him had stopped until he almost ran into him. He stumbled back a step, and Brother flowed up beside him to steady him.

"What's wrong?" Lod called ahead.

"Trail disappears," the man in the lead called back. "The damn goats might be able to go on, but we're not getting any further this way."

Lod frowned up at the mountainside.

The hunter peered around the men as well. High up on the peak ahead a trickle of smoke led them like a beacon. The dragon itself wouldn't be hard to find as long as it kept smoking. But the men were right. The trail ahead flattened against the slope, disappearing like a ripple on a pond. Any further that way and the men would risk breaking legs and ankles, or worse, falling to their deaths among the rocks below.

There was no point in losing good men before they even got up to the main threat.

Lod sighed loud enough to echo from the rocks around them. "We'll have to go back. Find another way up and around. Damn."

"Wait." The hunter held out a hand to forestall him.

"What is it?" Lod said.

"Let me try." He could feel the land under his feet. In the forest it had always felt like a faint singing, something he hadn't even noticed until Nan had pointed it out and made him practice listening to it. Here the rock seemed to mumble, like a restless sleeper.

Lod gestured him ahead, and the hunter climbed carefully around the other men to the head of the party. The trail dropped away leaving nothing but rocky scree and a steep slope, but the hunter closed his eyes and listened.

To the left the murmurs of the mountain faded into the open air, promising a swift death after a long fall. To the right the slope spoke in sharp whispers. It wouldn't be impossible, just very tricky.

The hunter placed his feet carefully, following the more gentle mumblings, trying to avoid the short sharp warnings of the treacherous rocks. Brother stepped carefully to follow him, planting his paws on the path the hunter laid out.

"Follow him," Lod said. "But carefully. Don't stray off the path he marks or you may start a rock slide."

The hunter climbed, inching along on tiptoes or dropping to all fours to lead the party of would be dragon slayers up the steep mountain. The trickle of smoke above grew steadily closer as the hunter's heart pounded faster and faster.

Were they climbing to their deaths? Brother was right, with no pack to watch their backs this was suicide. The men…they were better than no pack, but they didn't have the same rapport; they didn't have years of experience hunting together to mold them into a cohesive family.

Would it be so bad if they all died on this mountain? What else was left for them down in the valley? The hunter had already lost two families and the only human friend he'd ever made.

His fingers curled against the rocks under his hands. There were only two options for the end of this day. Either the slayer of the pack lay dead at his feet. Or he and brother would never have to worry about being lonely again.

The peak grew steeper and more treacherous the higher they got. A couple of snowflakes drifted past. It might be spring down below but up here, the last traces of winter bit at exposed skin. Just above the hunter's head, a ledge jutted into the open air, a trickle of smoke outlining it against the afternoon sky.

The hunter's shoulders tensed. The dragon.

He took a step without bothering to listen to the land, and his boot skidded against the loose rock.

He fell forward, catching himself on his hands as he slid down the slope a few feet.

The man behind him hissed and grabbed for his belt.

Brother yelped and lunged forward to drag the hunter up the slope.

The hunter dug his fingertips and toes into the mountain to keep from sliding any further.

"Quiet," Lod whispered from below. "Don't alert the dragon!"

A rumble shook the ground, making pebbles cascade down the slope around them. Smoke poured down over the edge of the ledge, choking them.

"Too late," a man called.

"Shit," the hunter muttered. There was nothing for it now.

He scrambled up the slope, finding desperate handholds among the rock. Just as he reached for the ledge, a massive shape barreled over head. The man behind him jumped back with a yell, lost his footing, and plummeted to the rocky crevice below.

The hunter gulped as the dragon pumped its huge wings and veered over them. He reached for the ledge again and hauled himself over. Brother scrambled after him. The hunter ducked as the dragon swooped overhead. Then he leaned over the ledge and offered his arm to the next man to help him climb up.

As soon as the huntsman was safely up, the hunter leaped to his feet and drew his knives.

The dragon roared, a great green-scaled storm of fury and teeth plunging at them over and over from the sky.

The hunter flailed wildly every time the beast swooped close, but he couldn't even begin to reach. Behind him, the rest of the men were still climbing up onto the ledge.

Finally Lod pulled himself over, just as the beast dove again.

The hunter saw the dragon's claws outstretched for the older man and he screamed and leaped for the vicious talons.

His blade barely scored the thick hide, but the dragon hissed and the claws clenched on empty air before it pumped its wings and curved away.

"We have to ground it," the hunter said. "Bring it down. We'll never get it while it's flying."

"Its wings," Lod called. "Aim for its wings."

The hunter sheathed his knives and pulled his bow from his back as the others spread out across the ledge, raising their bows to sight along arrows.

The dragon circled overhead and many of their arrows didn't make the distance, arcing harmlessly below the swooping monster.

The hunter raised his bow and sighted along his arrow, tracking the dragon's movement. Its wings cupped the air and the hunter counted, one, two, three, before releasing his arrow.

It streaked toward the dragon's wing and just as it heaved to flap again, tore a hole through the delicate membrane.

The dragon screamed.

"Aim before the upswing," the hunter called. He loosed arrow after arrow as Brother circled his feet.

Lod stepped up next to him with a longbow nearly as tall as he was.

With specific instructions more shots found their mark and the dragon faltered in its path.

"Duck," the hunter yelled as the beast lumbered into a turn and opened its jaws wide. He dove to the side as the stream of flame passed directly over the ledge. There was little cover here on the naked mountain top, and one of the other men stumbled over the edge, beating at the flames licking his arms and legs.

"Down, down," Lod mumbled, climbing to his feet beside the hunter.

"Yeah, but once its down, how do we keep it from knocking us all into the abyss?" the hunter said, gesturing to the edge of the ledge. There was nowhere to retreat to. Back down the mountain was nearly as treacherous as trying to continue up the last of the peak.

"We should have brought rope," Lod said.

The dragon came back for another pass but it dipped and shuddered in its flight and instead of another gout of flame it landed heavily on the ledge, plowing into the stone as if it had trouble controlling itself.

"Now," Lod called and the village huntsmen converged.

The hunter shook his head. "Wait."

The dragon's tail lashed around, throwing one of the men into the side of the mountain, and the hunter winced.

They might have grounded it but they'd never have a chance against the beast if they didn't contain it somehow.

Ropes, Lod had said.

Well, the hunter had the next best thing.

He reached toward the ground and then yanked up, pulling life from the earth itself. Vines sprang from the rock, showering them with pebbles as they snaked around the dragon's body.

The dragon thrashed as vines snapped closed, pinning its

wings to its body and its tail to the ground. It tried to shake itself like a wolf after a swim, but the hunter held the vines firm.

"Now, Lod," the hunter called.

Lod gave him a grateful nod and sprang for the dragon's back with his ax drawn. The others all found places to climb up the creature's limbs. Even Brother leaped to close his jaws on the dragon's snout.

The beast roared but could not break free.

The hunter watched, eyes going wide as the village huntsmen hacked the great animal to pieces.

This was what it deserved. It had killed the pack. It had killed Nan. In fire and fear it had destroyed half the valley, and it deserved to be put down.

But that didn't stop the hunter's stomach from clenching and acid crawling up his throat.

Blood flowed across the rock but the dragon still screamed and struggled.

He should want this. Why did it make him want to throw up?

He shook his head and tossed his bow to one side. Then he sprinted for the dragon's head. His muscles bunched, and he leaped to the beast's head, past Brother who clung desperately to its snout.

The hunter planted both knives deep in the dragon's eye.

The beast shuddered and lay still.

Tension dissolved from the hunter's shoulders and hands, and he tumbled from the dragon's head, rolling at the last minute to keep from breaking anything against the stone ledge. And then he lay there panting, fingers pressed into the cold rock beneath him as if that would keep the world from spinning.

The vines pulled away from the dragon's corpse and slithered back into the ground.

Brother jumped down beside him and came to lean his head into the hunter's side.

The hunter slung his arm around the wolf.

The rage that had sustained him the whole way up the mountain poured out of him, leaving nothing but an echoing cold.

The hunter knelt there with his face buried in Brother's fur as the village huntsmen cheered and kicked the dead dragon. They cavorted around the ledge, drunk on their victory and survival.

He concentrated on breathing trying to keep his breakfast down. Brother remained silent, breath warm against his cheek as the wolf panted.

Footsteps crunched on the loose gravel the vines had dislodged, and Lod crouched beside him.

The older man didn't say anything for a long moment.

"You all right?" he finally said. "Anything hurt."

The hunter shook his head, not trusting his voice right away.

"I don't—" He had to stop and swallow. "I don't know why I feel so sick. I've killed before. Plenty of times. I've killed to eat and I've killed to protect. But nothing has ever felt like this."

He turned his head just enough to see the bristle of Lod's beard out of the corner of his eye. "I wanted to slaughter that thing. It was all I could think about as we climbed. But as soon as the slaughter started, I just wanted it to stop."

Lod pulled off his hat and swiped his sleeve across his brow. The men still laughed and called out beyond them, but Lod seemed quiet. "This wasn't like killing to eat or survive. It protected others, sure. The valley is safe now. But it was also revenge for a lot of them." He gestured to the others.

The hunter grimaced and buried his head in Brother's fur again.

"It's not a bad thing to be averse to revenge. It's not a bad thing to keep your head in a fight when passion and grief should cloud it." Lod tilted his head back to the sky and closed his eyes as a couple of snowflakes settled in his beard.

The men began migrating toward the edge of the ledge, some carrying grisly trophies from their kill. Mostly scales and a few claws. They lowered themselves over the edge, taking care on the slippery slope.

"You coming back to the village?" Lod said. "This snow is going to get worse before it gets better. Best to be down by then."

"I don't…I don't know."

Lod nodded. "You did well today, boy," he said. "You'd make a good dragon hunter. And if you've no stomach for that after all this, you can always settle in the village. I need more huntsmen if we're going to survive another winter."

"I'll think about it," the hunter said. "I'll make my way down soon. I just…need a minute." He just needed time to think without the press of unfamiliar human voices. He needed the pack's warmth around him. But he wouldn't get that part.

"See you down there, then. Keep your footing."

Lod hesitated and then clapped him on the shoulder before following his men on their journey to the valley below.

The hunter waited until even the echoes of their passage faded before he finally turned to sit with his back against the dead dragon. Brother curled into his side.

What do we do now? he asked. He turned his nose up to the hunter.

"I don't know yet," the hunter said and rubbed his face. He still felt like he could be sick if he really wanted to, but at least now it wasn't hanging out in the back of his throat, threatening every breath.

Dragon hunter. The very word made the bile creep up his throat again. He hated the dragon that lay silent and dead behind him. That hate had sustained him the whole way up the mountain. But he couldn't even begin to imagine killing another one. The blood and ooze covering his hands made them tingle, and he couldn't wait to get to a stream or pond to rinse it off.

Killing the dragon hadn't brought his pack back to life. It didn't make Nan's death mean anything. It didn't even make him feel better. The opposite in fact.

So what was he supposed to do now? Hunting more dragons was clearly out. At least in terms of revenge. He had no stomach for a kill that meant nothing. Unless it was a way to protect others from a rampaging monster, he couldn't do it again.

Miraculously, he and Brother sat here alive. But they still had no pack. No family. No one to watch their backs, no one to grieve with or celebrate with or grow with. They still had each other, but that seemed somehow hollow when they both needed the stability of a pack working together.

Strange. The thought of family still brought up images of Father and the rest of the wolves, along with dim recollections of his actual parents. But it also stirred memories of Nan with her swift fingers and tart tongue.

Maybe he was ready for a more human family.

He could take Lod up on his offer. He could make his home in the village. It wouldn't be that bad would it? Nothing like the woods, of course.

But it didn't bring him comfort. Facing the villagers still made him want to hide. It made him extra aware of the cloak hanging from his shoulders. If he started wearing it now, after getting to know so many of them, they'd want to know why, and he could barely explain it to himself let alone to a group of nosy humans.

And while Lod was kind, the hunter wasn't ready to be a replacement son. The word was wrong, and he wasn't ready to find the right one.

It would all take too much fixing. And he didn't have the energy, not without Nan's wisdom.

He raised a hand to stroke Brother's head. At least it felt like his hand again instead of some numb piece he couldn't exactly control.

"We'll go back to the village for a little," the hunter said.

Brother's ears came forward.

"Just for a bit, to make sure they're okay. But I don't want to stay."

What do you want to do? Brother asked. *Go back to the woods?*

"I don't think we can go back there either. Not alone. It might be time to leave the valley."

Brother stood and shook himself, and the hunter prepared for an argument.

And then what? Brother said.

The hunter blinked. "That doesn't bother you?"

Not as long as we remain together. You are my pack, small as it may be. I will stay with you, guard you until we find a bigger pack, a bigger home and a place to belong.

The hunter bit his lip and buried his hand in the wolf's ruff as a sort of hug. "Yes," he said, voice thick. "That's what we'll do. And when we find one, we'll do better. We'll protect them. The way we couldn't with the pack."

Brother stood and shook the gathering snow from his fur. Then he hopped over the ledge and started his controlled skid down the mountainside.

The hunter stood and looked back at the dead dragon. He would not apologize to it. But he wanted to remember it. So the memory of it flaming the forest stood side by side with this dead thing which he had killed.

Then he pulled his hood over his head, allowing the deep pocket of fabric to hide his face. Until he was ready. Until he knew enough of who he was to show the world.

PART FIVE
SWAMP BEAST

The swamp monster's origin story is best read after *Magic and Misrule.*

NINE

A SCALY CREATURE stood at the edge of the meadow and watched the circus burn. Slime dripped from its underbite as panicked figures darted between flaming tents with buckets of water. The fire lit the night like a jewel in a puddle of murk.

This was beauty. This was perfection. This was what happened to those who tried to tame the swamp monster.

The beast master raced across the field, chased by a pair of lions, a baby wyvern, and one ancient baboon.

The swamp monster turned, the flames reflecting against its scales. Its skin shivered as if to shake free of the place, and it trotted into the trees at the edge of the meadow, leaving behind chaos. It's work here was done. Never again would it have to bow to masters stupid enough to leave a lit lantern in a tent filled with hay and a clever beast.

The swamp monster made its way through the forest, graceful and deadly and if there was no one around to see it trip over the tree roots, all the better.

The sun rose on the forest and the swamp monster lipped at the leaves of a nearby tree. It spat in disgust.

What was this? Freedom wasn't supposed to taste bitter. Where had the beast master gotten those sweet greens he had always fed it?

The swamp monster shook its head. It was resourceful and cunning. It should be able to find food easily. It didn't need some animal handler bringing dinner in a silver dish to survive.

It foraged up and down a stream bank, sampling the twigs and berries it found, spitting each one out as it found them.

Yuck, yuck, and more yuck. It deserved better than this.

The dry air itched in its nostrils, and it opened its mouth to pant.

Something scurried under a bush and in desperation, the swamp monster lunged. Its teeth clamped shut on a small furry body and it quickly swallowed it down.

Chipmunk al fresca. Better than nothing but hardly the first meal of freedom it had been expecting.

The swamp monster stalked through the underbrush, snapping up the small creatures that raced away from its clawed feet. It grumbled under its breath.

Something cracked, and it hissed before it realized the noise had been a branch under its feet.

Mucus dripped from its nose and it sniffled. Stupid forest. Wasn't nearly as comfortable as it had been led to believe. It needed moist air, not hot and dry. It needed scummy ponds and mossy trees. Snakes and fish would taste better than these furry little monstrosities.

It raised its snout and sniffed. There on the breeze it caught a whiff of moisture. Something that smelled far more green and inviting than this dinky stream.

It plunged through the trees following the scent of home. There was a swamp nearby, it just knew it.

A rope snapped around its neck and the swamp monster jerked to a stop, overbalancing and crashing into the forest floor.

It flailed, trying to get its feet under it.

"Whoa now. I'm sorry I startled you." A hand came into its field of view, offering it some help.

The swamp monster snapped, and its teeth drew blood.

"Ouch!"

The swamp monster surged to its feet, taking in the skinny man in the wide hat and the line of horses tied behind him.

The swamp monster hissed and yanked against the rope around its neck.

The man lunged to catch the end.

The swamp monster struggled, but the man dug in his heels.

After an entire day of exhausting freedom, the swamp monster was too weak with hunger to break free, and in just a few moments, it bowed its head, sides heaving.

The man reached a cautious hand to stroke the swamp monster's scales.

"There, there. It's all right. You're safe now."

The swamp monster snapped and almost got a finger as a reward.

Next time. Next time it would take off flesh.

That night, the swamp monster stood in a line with the other horses, watching as the man ate his stew. The firelight reflected in its eyes, a promise of things to come.

It ignored the pile of sweet greens in front of it—the same ones the beast master had always brought—and plotted.

The swamp monster would bide its time. It would gather its strength, and then it would leave these sorry excuses for horses and make its way into the swamp where it could live the life it was always supposed to live. It wasn't meant to live at the end of a rope, hand fed by inferior creatures. It was built to roam free, the terror of the swamp.

It wouldn't be that hard. The man looked pretty tippy. The swamp monster could probably push him into a puddle.

It raised its head toward the sky and waited.

ABOUT THE AUTHOR

Books have been Kendra's escape for as long as she can remember. She used to hide fantasy novels behind her government textbook in high school, and she wrote most of her first novel during a semester of college algebra.

Kendra writes familiar stories from unfamiliar points of view, highlighting different types of heroes.

When she's not writing she's reading, and when she's not reading she's playing video games.

She lives in Denver with her very tall husband, their book loving progeny, and a lazy black monster masquerading as a service dog.

Visit Kendra at
www.kendramerritt.com

facebook.com/kendramerrittauthor
twitter.com/Kendra_Merritt
instagram.com/kendramerrittauthor
goodreads.com/kendramerritt

Made in the USA
Columbia, SC
17 September 2022

67085709R00105